DAMAGED
A NOVEL

by
H.M. Ward

www.SexyAwesomeBooks.com
Laree Bailey Press

Laree Bailey Press
ISBN 978-0615796154
First Edition: April 2013

CHAPTER 1

Nerves shoot through my veins, filling my body with this spastic idea that it wants to run. Working hard to keep from fidgeting, I walk into the swank restaurant alone. Millie, my best friend, gave me some sob story this morning after we left the dorm room. Apparently, she met a hot new guy that wants to double-date tonight. My initial response was *Hell no*.

Last time she tried to set me up, I ended up on a date with a twitchy klepto. Let's just say things didn't go well. He picked up everything, except the check. The time before that was equally horrifying. I missed some verbal cue and my date ended the night with a face full of pepper spray.

Okay, maybe that was my fault. Maybe I'm too jumpy, too untrusting. The thing is, once something bad happens, there's no way to undo it. There's no erase button on life. I can't just click the delete key and start over. No matter how many guys I date, my brain is stuck on that night from long ago. Most days, my past follows me around like a thousand pound-bear on a piece of pink string, looming close enough to cast a shadow over everything I touch. But, once in a while, that beast rears up and mauls me. He slams me back to that horrible night and it's all I can do to not scream.

Dating provokes my past. It's almost as if I can hear the bear's claws clicking on the pavement behind me. My heart is beating too fast. My palms are damp with sweat. I want to get past this. I need to. It's been too long. My life is living me. I feel like I'm the one with a pink string around my neck. One mistake brought me to my knees. That's why I've shown up tonight. That's why I try. If I don't move forward, then I slide back, and I'm sick of reliving the past. I'm tired of the bear-sized baggage.

I want to move on with my life. I want to get over the fear that's choking me whenever I talk to a guy.

Determined to be different, I stand in front of the restaurant and try to work up more nerve and a fake smile along with it. The smile is lodged somewhere deep inside. I yank it out and plaster it across my face. It feels like plastic, stiff from misuse. I hate being fake. I hate this. My pulse pounds harder. I reach for the handle and finally look at the doors. They are made of hammered copper, with big wrought iron pulls. The metal feels cold in my hand. I yank the massive door open and step inside.

A wood carved hostess station is in front of me, with a beaming blonde behind it. She smiles at me. There are a few people waiting on padded benches, but it's not too busy right now.

I step forward and say, "I'm meeting up with someone. Can I see if they're already here?"

She nods and I walk past. The lighting is dim. The plaster walls are washed in rich warm colors. Dark drapes hang from oversized doorways, and a massive fireplace is in the center of the room. It has a stone chimney that stretches high into the copper ceiling.

I haven't been to this place before. Millie said she'd get there after me, but that Brent's friend, Dustin—my date—would be here first. I look for a lone guy sitting at a table for four that's about my age. I walk slowly around the room and no one fits the bill. I stand there for a moment, not knowing if I've been stood up, when I feel the hairs on the back of my neck prickle. Someone is looking at me. I feel their gaze on my back. I turn slowly and scan the room. A set of eyes, as blue as gemstones, gleam back at me. My stomach flutters. *Oh, holy hell, he's hot.* I walk slowly toward his table, barely breathing.

His eyes slowly slide over my body and he drinks me in. The way he does it is so sexual, so carnal, that my stomach twists. Butterflies fill me and career inside my stomach, growing swiftly to bat-sized with every step I take. The closer I get, the more nervous I feel. Is it possible that Millie set me up with someone this hot? I can't believe it. A soft smile lines my lips. It's not fake anymore. Our eyes are locked and I can't look away. My heels click in time with my heartbeat and suddenly I'm standing in front of him at the table.

"Hey," I manage to say, still looking into his eyes. They're so vibrant. It's as if someone painted him. He's perfect. If his voice matches his looks, I'll melt into a puddle on the floor. Dustin's quite the looker.

The corner of his mouth lifts and I'm treated to a swoon-worthy smile. "Hey, yourself." Oh, his voice. It's hotter than I thought. There's a richness to the tone. Add in the smirk and the dimple and it feels as though my knees are going to give out. I know I can't do anything with him—maybe—but he's the most delicious eye candy I've had in a long time. The way he looks at me is making me hot. I place my hands on the chair opposite him and slide it out. His eyes remain on me, watching me as I sit down across from him.

I don't know what to say, so I smile back at him and resort to clichés. "So, you come here often?"

"You know it," he says, still looking at me. It's as if he can't believe that I'm sitting in front of him. The intense gaze makes my stomach twist. This guy is beyond beautiful. Dark locks of perfectly messy brown hair sweep across his face, with a few longer pieces by his eyes. An insane urge to lean forward and feel how smooth and silky his hair is between my fingers shoots through me. I shove the sensation back down. The man sitting in front of me isn't one of those Texas boys that's all talk. This guy has hardly said anything and I'm enthralled.

The waiter comes and asks if I want to order. I ask for a glass of wine. When the waiter leaves, a moment passes in steamy silence. My eyes keep drifting to his broad chest and those full, beautiful, lips. It concerns me. I mean, this affect he has on me is like magic. I'm turning into a hot mess and he's barely said two words. I break the silence and look up at him as I put my napkin on my lap. "You know, you're nothing like I thought you'd be."

"Really?" he asks, now grinning at me.

I nod shyly, and the waiter returns with the glass of wine. I take a sip as he says, "So, tell me what you think now."

A coy smile lines my lips. I feel girlish, but the wine makes me brave. I shrug and look at him from under my lashes. "I think tonight is going to be a good night."

"It's going to be interesting, to say the least." He carries himself so differently than most of the guys around here. He's self-assured. There's a slant to his shoulders that tells me he's confident, erring on cocky. He leans back in his side of the booth, watching me. His dazzling eyes remain on my face, and his eyebrow twitches once in a while as I speak.

I'm so nervous that I can't shut up. "Yeah, it is. This is the first time I've been in here. I never come over to this side of town. Everything is so far away. There'd be four towns crammed into this space back home, but I suppose that's what makes Texas, Texas—the sprawling land."

He nods. "Texas can be like that. Do I detect a slight accent from you—uh, I'm sorry, what was your name?"

I laugh. A slight accent is an understatement. I'm all accent. "Sydney."

He leans forward with a quizzical look in his eyes. "You're from Australia? No way." A smile spreads across his face and I know he's teasing. "I thought they only talked that way in Jersey." He winks and grins at me.

I laugh. He's caught me off guard. I expected my date tonight to be disastrous, but this guy seems perfect. In the back of my mind, I wonder where Millie is and I'm glad she's late. I'm having fun smiling and flirting with him. The tension eases out of me the longer I sit with him. It's amazing. He's peeling back the layers and drawing out the girl I used to be. "My name is Sydney. I'm from Cherry Hill in New Jersey, wise ass."

"I'm pleased to meet you, Sidney. You brightened an otherwise dreadfully dreary night." He raises his glass and nods before taking a drink. It's a flattering, here's-to-you movement that makes me want to know more about him. I mean, who does that? He's different and I admire that.

I glance at him for a second. I like the way he looks at me. I like the way he says my name. I like him. "Glad I could be of service. I'm all about the chivalry." My fingers pull my silverware toward me and I unfold it and put the napkin on my lap.

He laughs. "I can see that."

Millie's voice rings out behind me. "Sidney? There you are! We're all sitting on the other side of the restaurant. I've been calling you." Millie is wearing a cute little dress with a swishy skirt. She gives me a look and stands there with her hands on her hips, as if I've been bad.

I smile at my date and then back at Millie, not getting it. I look up at her, wondering why she doesn't slip into the booth next to me. "I turned my phone off when I came in. I couldn't have it ringing while I was talking to this fine man, could I? Come on, Millie. Sit down. I'm sure Brent will be here any second." I look past her to see if he's here yet.

Mille shakes her head. She has a smile of disbelief on her face. She leans closer to me. "Brent's already here, you lunatic. Now

come away and leave this nice man alone."
She looks up at him and then back at me.

The smile fades from my lips. I look at
Millie, pulse pounding, and then back at the
beautiful man across the booth. Horror
slips over me like a cold sheet and I go
rigid. I look at his shoulder. I can't meet his
eyes. "You're not my date, are you?" He
shakes his head, still smiling at me. My face
flames red at the same time that my eyes
elegantly bug out of my head. For some
reason, he offends me. I mean, I was sitting
here with him for how long and he didn't
bother to say that I had him mistaken for
someone else?

I get louder and squeak as I scold him.
"When were you going to tell me?"

He shrugs, seemingly amused, and rubs
the dusting of stubble on his beautiful jaw.
"I thought you were trying to pick me up."
My mouth forms an O and I stare at him
for a second, unable to blink. My hands
quickly cover my face and I chant, *oh my god,*
oh my god, to myself under my breath. I hear
his voice and see his smile when I look up.
"You were doing a pretty good job. I would
have been happy to buy you dinner."

That doesn't make things better.

Millie's looking at me like I'm nuts. I feel her hand around my wrist, pulling me up. I stand and follow her away from the table. I can't stop blushing. I can't get rid of the stupid feeling that's choking me. I want to crawl under a table and hide. I feel Hot Guy's eyes on me as I walk away. I don't look over my shoulder. I can't, but God, I want to. He's so perfect. Why does this stuff happen to me?

CHAPTER 2

I've never been in this restaurant before. When I came in, I thought I'd circled the entire floor, and seen every table, but I hadn't. This section is behind the wall that connects to the bar. I didn't realize there were tables over here, and apparently this is where Mille and the guys have been sitting.

Millie has been talking, but I'm so mortified that I'm not really listening. She finally stops at a booth on the other side of the fireplace and scoots in next to Brent. My date pats the spot beside him. Oh God. He looks like my ex. My nerves are frayed as it is, and the similarities between the two men are so striking that I flinch. Old memories flash behind my eyes. The memories feel fresh, as though they just happened. I don't want to sit down. I want to run. My fingers graze the scar hidden under my necklace. I'm frantic, and maybe a little terrified.

Stop it! I scold myself. This guy didn't hurt you. Sit down. I chant *sit down* over and over again inside my head. I can't let fear rule my life. It's held me back long enough. I'm getting over it—tonight. There have been too many times that I've let my past crush me. I managed talking to hot guy a few moments ago. I can figure this out. I can be the girl I was before. I swallow hard and sit down. Millie spares me and doesn't mention that she found me at a random table, chatting up a hot guy.

I try to shake off what just happened so I can focus on my real date. When I see him, dread tries to crawl up my throat.

Millie introduces us after I sit down. "Sydney, this is Brent and his friend, Dusty."

Dusty's a pretty cowboy. He's got his hair slicked back and parted on the side. He's wearing a starched white Western shirt. I bet he's got fancy cowboy boots under the table, too—the kind that cost more than my car.

I sigh and say, "Hello." I try not to think that tonight just got a million times worse, but I can't help it. I've been on this date before – at least I think I have. The choking sensation returns. My spine stiffens. Being this close to him has me on edge. Mentally, I scold myself to calm down, but it doesn't work. I can't. Every muscle in my arms and legs is corded tight, ready to run.

Nervously, I smile at him again and take my napkin off the table. I spread it across my lap. The little black dress I'm wearing has a scoop neck that dips low in front. The bodice clings to my curves and the skirt flares at the waist. I feel pretty, but the way his eyes rove over me makes me feel nervous.

I shift in my seat and glance at Millie. She's already gushing, batting her eyelashes at Brent. It's amazing that she can sit so close to me and be in her own little world. Brent is wrapped up in her, too.

"So," Dusty says—his eyes overtly drifting to my breasts before reluctantly returning to my face—like I'm good enough, "it's a good thing it's not raining tonight."

"And why's that?"

He grins at me and says, "Because sugar melts in the rain." Dusty pours on the country accent and smiles at me with a wolfish grin.

My eyebrows lift. I feel them inch up my face until they disappear under my bangs. I smile and laugh, nervously, not able to say anything that Millie won't kill me over later. A sudden urge to run screaming from the table shoots through my body. Maybe the kitchen will catch fire and I can leave. I glance in that direction, hopeful.

Millie and Brent are talking. They're both leaning into one another, as if they can't get enough of each other. Millie giggles at something Brent says, and then looks at me. I smile at her for a second, before her attention returns to Brent.

I press my back into the seat, wishing I was somewhere else. But I'm here. I'm here for Millie. I'm here for me. Taking a deep breath, I try to reign in my nerves before they get the better of me.

I feel Dusty's eyes on the side of my face. They dip too low and I know he's looking at my chest, again. I wiggle in my seat, scooting away from him and closer to the edge of the booth.

Dusty leans back in the seat and asks, "So, what's your major?"

Nerves are flopping through my stomach like drunken bats. I'd give anything to trade them for butterflies right now. I'm so nervous. I feel so sick, but I refuse to leave. I have to do this. I have to have a normal date, get through a normal night. If I can do that, I can get on with my life. Just eat dinner, kiss the guy, have sex, and go home. That's what my friends do. I can do that. I can. The bear raises his head and gives me a look. Fucking bear.

I take too long to answer. Dusty lightly touches the back of my hand. He traces his finger in a circle and says, "It's okay if you're undecided. I was just starting with the basics."

Don't yank your hand away. My heart pounds harder. My ribs are going to crack. I find my fake smile and giggle nervously. "I'm not undecided. I'm an English major. What's your major?"

"Business." Dusty tries to gaze into my eyes, but whenever I look at him, the pit of my stomach turns to ice. God, I'm a wreck. It was easier to talk to that other guy.

I force my gaze up and smile at him again, even though I'd rather bang my head on a rock. "So, do you want to start a business?"

"Something like that. Maybe open a shop or manage one of my dad's stores. I don't really know yet. After I finish this, I have to do graduate work, so it's still a 'ways off." He lifts his arms and slips it behind me.

I can't breathe. It's as though he knocked me in the back with a two-by-four. When his arm settles over me, it's even worse. Damn it. Why can't I sit here? Why does every touch have to make me so crazy? I'm getting better, I swear to God I am.

Then why are you still acting like this? That little voice in the back of my head is a total bitch. She's in cahoots with the bear.

Brent nods, and continues talking to Millie about a class they had earlier today. Millie laughs.

Dusty rubs his fingers on the edge of my shoulder, touching my bare skin. The dress is sleeveless. Suddenly, I'm somewhere else, lost in a memory. I feel my ex's hands on me. The past and the present crash together. I stiffen more. "Relax. I won't bite. And Brent can vouch for me. I'm not a total ass—"

"His ass-o-meter rating is around a two. No worries there, Sidney." Brent smirks at me. His eyes slip over his friend's arm around my shoulders. "Me, on the other hand—"

Millie slaps his chest and laughs, "You're perfect. I wouldn't change a thing." She leans in and kisses him. My face flushes and I look away. Mistake. When I do it, Dusty is watching. Our eyes lock, but it's not a good feeling. It evokes everything I want to forget.

The waiter saves me, and Millie stops sucking face long enough to order. We share an appetizer. Dusty talks more about his family and home. He pops a piece of shrimp into his mouth. "What about you? Did your family support you coming down here?" Somehow Dusty has closed the gap between us. We're shoulder to shoulder, hip to hip. There's no way to scoot away from him, either. One more wiggle and I'll fall on the floor.

When he mentions my family, I feel my hackles raise. It's a common enough question, so I try to sound normal. "Yeah, of course. Whose family wouldn't want them to go to college? And this school's great." I'm distracted. I lie. My stupid family doesn't even know where I am.

Dusty leans in close to me. He takes a curl between his fingers. I glance at him and twist so the curl drops. "You look so hot tonight." My eyes instantly avert their gaze. Even though I'm no longer looking at him, I can feel Dusty's eyes on my skin. The hairs on the back of my neck prickle. He leans in toward me and places his hand on my knee, slowly. Very slowly. I won't react. I can do this. I can. It's a normal touch.

It's normal. I want to be normal. I want it so badly, but my eyes sting. My pulse is pounding like someone is chasing me with an axe. I smile at him again, forcing myself to stay put. Dusty takes my smile the wrong way. His hand slips under the hem of my dress and halfway up my thigh—skin to skin—and squeezes. He grabs me and my world shifts. I'm here, but my mind is lost in the past, reliving memories that I want to forget.

My muscles react without my consent. Shooting out of my seat, I jump up, banging into the table, shaking all the silverware. It makes a loud noise. I hold out my hands, ready to make up some excuse, when I whirl around and slam into a waiter. He's holding a tray of food—our food— high over his head. When I slap into him, the tray topples to the side. Every entrée slips to the side in slow motion, and slides off the side of the tray. There's a loud crash when the plates hit the floor.

For a second, I stand there paralyzed. Dusty gives me a *what the hell* look. Millie and Brent follow suit. I feel their stares and can't explain. They don't know. My mouth dangles open, but I don't know what to say.

I bolt. Before the night can get any worse, before I can make a bigger an ass out of myself, I leave. I walk swiftly toward the exit, ready to scream or cry—maybe both. What the hell is wrong with me? I wanted this. I'm the one who let him do it. It's like last time. The images flash through my mind, but tears are blinding me. I push through the massive doors, and nearly trip over the curb.

When the night air hits my face, I slow down. No one is chasing me. None of them want me to come back. I inhale deeply. The last half an hour has been an emotional rollercoaster. First, I humiliate myself, and then I get grabbed. I cringe inwardly. I'm so stupid.

As I dig through my purse for my keys, standing under the portico, I glance up and my heart lurches. It's the hot guy. He's in the parking lot with his hands on his hips, in front of a black car. The way he stands draws attention to his broad shoulders and trim waist. I drink him in before I notice that the hood is up. Why was I able to talk to him? That guy didn't make me panic at all. I felt like the old me and not the lunatic that I've become. I miss who I was. I miss the old me. I know she's still inside somewhere, locked away.

He must sense eyes on him, because he turns and sees me. Raising his voice so that I can hear him, he says, "I take it that neither of us is having a good night?"

I stare at him for a moment. My heart is still pounding. I'm in danger of stroking out. Before I can think about what I'm doing, I nod and walk toward him. Stopping next to Hot Guy, I say, "It was total suckage." Some of the tension leaves my shoulders. This guy—whoever he is—has that old friend feeling. I don't understand it. It feels as if I've known him for years even though I don't know his name. It's weird.

I sigh and look at his engine. "Car trouble?"

Running his fingers through his hair, he says, "It appears that way. It won't start and it isn't from lack of trying."

Folding my arms across my chest, I watch the way he's looking at the car and can tell that he doesn't know what he's looking at. Neither do I, really, but I know a little. I walk to the driver's side door, pull it open, and sit in the seat.

He watches me as I try to crank the engine. It doesn't start. I look at the little gauges and notice the battery. He's standing next to me now. "So, you're a mechanic?"

I shake my head, "I just pretend to be. It makes for more interesting evenings." I grin at him, not sure what's come over me. I never talk random guys, but it's not like he's random anymore, right? Hot Guy's face falls and I realize that he believes me. I laugh, "I'm just kidding. I know a little about cars. For instance, I know this one isn't going anywhere tonight."

"And why's that?"

"It seems like your alternator's dead. Either that or you shoved a hamster up the tailpipe—" My face falls. I wonder if he did something stupid. College guys do all sorts of stupid things to talk to girls. I get out of his car and slam the door. Then, I tilt my head and cross my arms over my chest. "Tell me that that isn't the reason the car won't start."

He laughs and presses a hand to his chest, shocked that I'd say such a thing. "No, I didn't do anything like that! And correct me if I'm wrong, but you were the one who came onto me first. I didn't get here early and sabotage my own car, just so I could meet a girl I didn't know was coming." The way he smiles is contagious. He runs his hands through his dark hair, like he wishes he could say more, but he doesn't. The corners of his mouth curve and he gives me a look that makes tingles crawl across my skin.

I step toward him, smiling too wide. "I did not come onto you!"

"You did. Right back in there." He points toward the restaurant. His face is serious, all smooth features and big blue eyes. "You sat at my table and made me very uncomfortable. I haven't had such a beautiful woman overtly hit on me like that before. It was quite embarrassing."

My smile is making it hard for my mouth to hang open in shock. It keeps opening and then my grin snaps my lips shut. "I did not!" I know he's teasing me, but I can't stop. I don't want it to stop, and I realize that I'm actually laughing.

His arms are folded over his chest. He taps a finger to his lip, as if he's remembering. "You did. You ordered wine and just assumed that I'd put out. Really, Sidney, you'll have to learn to control yourself a little better in the future." He looks at me from the corner of his eye, as he glances at his car.

I know he's baiting me, but I can't ignore him. I can't walk away and I don't want to. He smiles at me with those wicked lips. It makes me want to kiss him, hard. I change tactics. I want to throw him so far off balance that he falls over. I step in front of him and look up at him from under my lashes. "Okay, you caught me. I like you. I want you. I can't keep my hands off of you. But tell me this, beautiful man; why should I bother controlling myself when I can tell that you want me just as much?" Slowly, I step closer to him. Our bodies are a breath apart as I look up into his eyes.

Smiling, he manages to say, "You shouldn't." He watches me, waiting to see what I'll do. I feel my heart pounding. His eyes drift to my lips and back to my eyes. Every inch of my body flickers to life. I want to feel his hands on me. I want his lips on my mouth. From the look in his eye, I know he wants it too.

I lean in closer, teasing him. I feel his breath on my lips. His scent fills my head and I breath him in. "Are you always this irresistible?"

"Are you always this coy? Do you just flirt, leaving your lips way too close to a man that desperately wants to kiss you?"

My hands drift to his hair as he speaks. I touch him gently and hear his breath hitch. It sends a thrill through me, making me brave. There's little space between us. The tension is so strong that I can't stand it another second. I lean in slowly and brush my lips to his. Beautiful Man stands there. He seems surprised. He doesn't move. He doesn't kiss me back. Disappointment floods me. I look down, breaking the kiss. I can't hide how hard I'm breathing, how much he turns me on.

Rejection doesn't look good on me. "I'm sorry," I breathe. I'm about to turn away when I feel his fingers tilt my chin up. I look him in the eye, and see something there that I didn't expect.

He's smiling softly. "Don't be. I just like to be on a first name basis with the random girls that I suck face with in swank parking lots."

I smile. "I didn't realize the parking lot was swank, too."

"It is. And Miss Sidney, if you'd be so kind as to divulge your last name?"

"Who talks like that?" I laugh.

"I believe that I do."

"Sidney Colleli." I bit my bottom lip and look up at him.

"Peter Granz." His voice is deep and rich. The way he says his name makes my insides melt, and the way he kisses is even better. Gently, Peter pulls my lips back to his, and he kisses me lightly. It sends a charge through my body and makes my toes curl. I lean into him, loving the way he feels. Every part of me is tingling, wanting more. The kiss is so light, so brief. When Peter pulls away, I can barely breathe.

In a breathy voice, I say, "It's nice to meet you."

CHAPTER 3

I glance back at the restaurant, worried that my date will come through those doors at any second. Eager to leave, I glance at Peter and ask, "Would you like a ride home?"

Peter nods and says, "That'd be great."

I grin. A girlish giggle bubbles up inside me and I swallow it whole. I'm going to be alone with a gorgeous guy in my car! I can't feel my brain. It left my body during that kiss.

Peter follows me across the parking lot and back to my car. We both slip inside and I start the engine. I navigate my way through the parking lot and when I pull out onto the road, I ask, "Which way?"

He smiles at me sheepishly. "I don't know. I just got here." The smile on his face is stunning. He looks so boyish and perfect.

I laugh and glance at him. "You don't know where you live?"

"I know where I live. I just don't know where it is in relation to here. I just moved here."

"Oh, how long have you been in town?"

Peter smiles sheepishly. "A few weeks, but this is my first time over here. The town is sprawling. I admit that I didn't pay attention on the way over, and my sense of direction is less than stellar. I've been using the GPS in my car to get around. I start a new job tomorrow and ran out to grab something to eat. Fast food was getting old. I heard about this place and decided to try it. Then, I met you and the rest is history." Peter has an easy way about him. He leans back into the seat and looks out the window. He points east and says, "I think I live that way."

I can't stop laughing. "The dump is that way. There's nothing else over there."

Peter's dark brows pull together as he looks out the window and then back at me. "Are you sure? I thought the apartment looked rather nice when I left." He leans forward and looks out the window. It's dark. The sky is inky with the normal spattering of white stars. The only décor on the sides of the road are mesquite trees that jut up from the ground like bony fingers and brittle, dried-out, grass.

Pulling out, I ask, "What's the name of your apartment complex?" I try to drive slowly so I won't miss the on-ramp, if I need to hop on the highway.

"It's called Ridgewood, or something like that. It's across the street from the college." Peter's looking at me. I can feel his eyes on the side of my face. I don't mean to, but I pull my bottom lip into my mouth again and nibble on it. The heat from his gaze makes me nervous. When he speaks, his voice is so deep that it sends ripples through me. "Keep doing that and I'm going to kiss you."

"We're driving," I say, and look over at him, freeing my lip.

"I didn't say it was smart. I just said I'd have to do it. Your lips are amazing, and when you do that it makes me want to nibble them, too." Heat spreads across my cheeks, along with an insane smile. Peter grins at me. "How cute. You blush."

"Shut up," I laugh, waiting for my cherry red cheeks to go away.

"No, it's sweet. I like it."

He stops talking, as we pull into his parking lot. Peter lives about five minutes from the restaurant. It was probably the first thing he saw when he came into town.

"Which one?" I ask, trying to decide which way to turn. The complex is huge. Some of my friends live over here since it has a volleyball court, a club house, and a pool. Me and Millie live in the dorms and can only dream of an apartment like these.

"That way." He points, and I drive around to the back of the complex. Peter presses his lips together into a thin line and then looks back at me. "Do you want to come inside for a cup of coffee?"

I stare at him for a moment. Damn, he's so beautiful. I want to get to know him better, but I can't tell what he's asking for and it's late. I'm not into one-night stands, and I have enough issues when it comes to guys. Besides, I want someone to be mine when we go all the way. I sound like a high school student. Or a 50's remnant. Maybe we can go steady, too, and that would be groovy. My mind is all over the place.

Mid-freakout, I glance at him. "Is that code for sex or are we really having coffee?"

Peter laughs and feigns shock, putting his hand over his chest. "My God! Is that why all those women at Starbucks keep trying to have *coffee* with me?"

I slap his shoulder and shake my head. The smile on my face hasn't faded since we got in the car. I pull into a parking spot and we both get out. I follow him to the second floor because I can't let him think that I don't want his coffee, not after that whole Starbucks comment. We chat about nothing and he teases me more. I tease back. It feels natural. It's not fake and I'm not scared. I'm so sick of being alone all the time. One event set my life on a different course. I want to change it back. I want to pull out of this nose-dive and get on with things. I'm damaged goods and I know it.

Peter reaches into his pocket and fishes out his keys. I watch him as he does it. His shoulders are strong and muscular. They lead into a hard torso with a trim waist. I think about running my fingers over his stomach, and feeling my fingertips trace the taut muscles.

Peter looks back at me as he opens the door. He smiles, like he knows what I was thinking about, and says, "After you."

I step inside his apartment and see boxes everywhere. Some are unpacked, but most have the tops torn open, as though he was looking for something before he ran out the door. "Welcome to my shabby abode."

"It's not shabby. And it's so much nicer than the dump. You just need to unpack." I glance around. There's a couch shoved against the wall. Peter walks into a little kitchen off the living area and starts the coffee.

"Are you hungry?" he calls to me. "Did you get to eat anything? You looked pissed when you walked out. I'm guessing that you didn't get a chance." Peter's standing in the doorway. I turn toward him. He noticed a lot more than I thought.

"It's okay. The coffee's fine."

"Ah, *coffee*," he says, and winks at me.

"Not like that! Oh my God, you're so..." I laugh and navigate my way through the boxes to the couch.

Sticking his head out of the kitchen, he holds onto the wall and says, "So what? So lovable? So manly? So sexy? So—"

"So irritating!" Of course I don't mean it. Every time I stop smiling, he lights me up again like a Christmas tree.

"Ah. I was hoping you were going to say 'so sexy—totally beddable.' I could live with that." He winks and disappears back into the kitchen. Before I can reply, he tells me, "Well, I have some cold cuts in here. I'll bring you a sandwich. Just give me a second." I hear him moving around and decide not to protest. I am hungry. I didn't get to eat anything except that wine, and wine as dinner usually isn't a good plan.

I make myself comfortable on his couch, kick off my heels, pull my feet under me, and curl into the arm of the couch. It smells like him. I rest my face against the soft suede and breathe the scent in. It's musky and masculine. God, he smells good. If couches were sexy, this one would be a cover model. Pressing my nose to the arm, I inhale deeply.

Peter chooses that moment to reappear, plate in hand, and stops. He's staring at me with an amusedly shocked expression on his face. "Are you sniffing my couch?"

"No!" I sit up fast, too fast. I panic. He's staring at me like I'm a freak. I probably am, I mean I was snorting the guy's couch. I need a diversion. Anything. I reach into my brain and pull out the only thing that's there.

Using my best bedroom voice, I wink at him and ask "Can I distract you with some coffee?"

Peter's face glows when he laughs. He takes the few steps forward and hands me the plate. I gratefully take it. For a brief moment, I consider pulling the sandwich apart and hiding behind the bread. The way Peter is looking at me doesn't help the rosy glow on my face. I got caught sniffing his couch. God, I can't think of anything worse than that. He probably thinks I escaped from the asylum.

We stay quiet too long, which makes me nervous. Between bites, I ask him the basics. "So, you don't sound like a hick, but I can't tell where you're from."

"Connecticut. Yankee-ville, same as you, little Miss Jersey."

"You moved down here for work?"

Peter nods. "Yeah. It was time for a change of pace." He looks away from me when he says it, his eyes dropping to the floor. There's more there, something heavy, but I don't press him. "This place came up on the grid, and I thought Texas would be different, so I went for it and managed to piss off my entire family. That was a bonus." He tilts his head at me before sitting down on the couch.

"Yeah, my family was mad when I came down here, too. They gave me the old Italian guilt about abandoning my family... Like they can't function without me?" I bite my sandwich and shake my head. "My family is so tight that none of us can breathe without someone else knowing about it. I was glad to get out of there. I needed space." I finish the sandwich and look for a spot to put the plate.

"I know what you mean." Peter smiles at me and takes the plate from my hand. "Honestly, you're the first person I've spoken to down here that I get along with. Everyone else seems as if they escaped from a movie set."

"I know, right? I said that to Millie when I first moved down here. Actually, I said it to a group of people. Millie was the only one who laughed, which made her quality friend material. The rest of the people scowled at me."

"Millie is the girl that came to get you from my table?" Peter asks, before he goes into the kitchen to grab the coffee.

I nod. When he walks back out of the kitchen, I ask, "Hey, what were you planning on doing when I figured out that you weren't my blind date?"

Peter brings me a cup of coffee and sits down next to me again. "I didn't know you thought you were on a blind date. I figured it out when you did, maybe a second sooner. The look on your face was so adorable. I'm glad you stopped and said something when you came outside." Peter looks at me over the top of his mug as he sips his coffee. Those blue eyes are intoxicating. I can't stop staring at him.

We talk about nothing for a while longer, until I put my cup down on a box next to me. The entire time we chat, I feel pulled to him. There's something there, something about him that holds onto me and connects deeper than I've connected with anyone—and for some reason I'm not afraid. I don't know what it is, exactly.

Peter has an easy way about him. That smile lights up his entire face when he flashes it at me. Yet, there's a haunted look behind his eyes, like his life has been harder than he lets on. I sense it in him. Like calls to like and my life has been anything but easy. When I find another person who has that fragile, battered, spirit, I instantly relate. The thing is, there aren't that many of them. I don't know if other people lay down and die when things go wrong or they harden so much they're no longer alive. I refuse to bend, refuse to turn to stone. The pain in my life won't destroy me. I won't let it. I see the same conviction in his eyes and hear it in his voice. There's something he left behind, someone who scarred him. The pleasantries, that cocky grin and those dazzling eyes, try to hide it from me, but I know it's there. He's damaged like me. It pulls me to him in a way that's too powerful to ignore.

Peter reaches past me and sets his empty cup on the same box. His arm brushes against mine as he does. I breathe him in. God, he smells good. That pull between us gets even stronger. When he straightens, we're sitting very close. Peter's sapphire eyes lock with mine and my stomach goes into a free fall. This is it. I can feel it. I can sleep with this guy and erase the last one. I've already come this far. It's a few more steps, a few more minutes. I can do this. I can.

Besides, the guy makes me feel as though I can actually be with him. I want to touch him, which is so strange. I haven't felt like this in a really long time. It's as if he brought me back to life. And right now, it's all I can do to sit here and not thrust my fingers into his hair. I want to feel him against me. I want that kiss on his lips, the one that he's been teasing me with all night. Peter's breath crosses my cheek when he exhales. It's warm and perfect. My heart races faster as he moves closer to me. His eyes study my face, taking in every detail. Nerves twist my stomach in giddy anticipation.

Peter lifts his hands and strokes his fingers along one side of my face, gently caressing my cheek. My eyes close in response, and I lean into his hand. Every part of me flutters to life. My voice is caught in my throat. I can't speak. I feel the tension building between us and I'm going to melt. I want to melt. I want to stop thinking for a while, I want to move on with my life and lose myself in his kiss. This is so weird for me, but I don't pull away. I force myself forward.

Heat shoots through my body and I feel myself inching toward him, wanting to taste his kiss, wanting to hold him against me. Peter's fingers brush my hair away from my face, and he dips his head and covers my lips with his. I suck in a jagged breath, unable to hide how much he affects me. Peter's bottom lip brushes against mine. He kisses me softly, hesitantly at first. Each kiss is slow and tentative, wanting to know if I want more. Nipping my bottom lip with his teeth, Peter kisses me and I respond. I lean into him and press my mouth roughly against his. I feel his tongue brush the seam of my lips, asking for them to part. He sweeps against them lightly once, twice, and I open my mouth. Brushing his tongue along the curves of my mouth, Peter kisses me deeper. I moan, leaning into him, not wanting it to stop. Every part of my body is burning up. Every bit of me is hypersensitive to his touch. As his hands touch my skin, I feel lighter, like I'm floating.

I press myself closer to Peter, and trail my fingers up his back, feeling the curves of his toned body. Peter's hands respond by drifting lower to my waist and slipping under the hem of my shirt. When he touches me, it feels good. My pulse races. I can't slow it. I can't hide my rapid breaths or what he's doing to me. Peter's touch sets me on fire. I pull him down on top of me, and we lay back on his couch. His lips don't stop and neither do mine.

I've never responded this way before. I've had hot kisses before, but this isn't the same. This is a connection that runs deeper. His kiss shoots through me like an arrow, catching on the anchor that weighs down my soul. There are few times that I'm certain of anything, and now is one of them. Peter Granz is different. Everything from his touch to his voice draws me to him.

My fingers work at the buttons on his shirt. When I push back the fabric, it falls to the floor to reveal a chiseled chest and rock hard abs. I gasp, and run my fingers over the contours of his body. Peter watches me as I slide my hand across his chest and trail my fingers down to his stomach. When I hit his waistband, I slow my hand and glance at his eyes.

"You're beautiful," he breathes. Lowering his head, Peter dips and presses a slow kiss to my neck. I close my eyes and enjoy the sensations shooting through my body. His hands move over the bodice of my dress, slowly testing how far he can go. When his palm brushes over my breast, I moan into his ear. My hips push into his and I can feel how hard he is, how much he wants me.

Peter's kisses trail down my neck, leaving a hot wake behind. His mouth is so hot. Every time he presses a kiss to my skin, my back lifts off the couch. I can't stay still. Everything he does makes me respond. My hands find his back and sweep over his muscles. They're so tense, so hard. Peter shifts his weight, moving one leg to the side. Watching me, he touches the neckline of my dress, slowly pushing the shoulder strap down. Breathing slow and deep, I watch him. His eyes darken as he looks at me. His fingers gently pull the other strap until it comes loose. I feel his eyes on me. I know that I want this. Peter slips down the top of my dress.

I'm wearing a sheer black bra. He can see everything. Peter's eyes drink me in as though he could never get enough, before lowering his head to my breast. His lips move over the fabric at first, teasing me, making my nipples so hard that they ache.

Rational thought has left my body. I'm moaning beneath him, pressing myself against him. This feels right and I want this. I want to feel his lips on me. I want to feel his tongue flick against me. I moan and tangle my hands in his dark hair. My back arches and thrusts me harder against his mouth. Peter's hands move to my straps. He slips off one strap and exposes the soft skin beneath.

Peter kisses my bare shoulder. His mouth drifts lower, burning a path of hot kisses to my breast. I feel his hand, hot and heavy, pass over the curves. He holds me for a moment, feeling me against his hand. Peter's thumb brushes my nipple making my hips move on their own. Breathing hard, I say his name, begging him to kiss me, to touch me there. His lips brush against my skin and I melt. My entire body responds to him. Every inch of me is on fire, hot, wanting—no needing—him. Peter kisses and nips me until I'm lost in a thick haze of lust. My hips rock against his, wanting more.

That's when he lowers a hand to my leg and traces his finger slowly up my inner thigh. My legs fall open. I suck in a breath, wanting his hand to slip under my dress, to that hot spot between my legs. Peter moves slowly, watching me. His hand brushes over the outside of my panties, touching me lightly. The movement makes me crazy. I can't stand the way Peter teases me, how he watches me like he knows what he's doing to me. My nails find his forearms and scratch. It's as if that action breaks what's left of Peter's self-control, and in seconds he's on top of me, pressing me harder into the couch. His hand is between my legs and his lips are on my breast. I writhe against his hand, with a thousand different sensations shooting through my body.

Everything is perfect until a startlingly loud sound breaks the spell. The phone in the kitchen rings, echoing in the empty apartment. Peter stops moving. The jarring noise won't end. It keeps ringing and ringing. Peter sighs into my shoulder. We're both still for a moment, until he pushes up.

Peter sits on the end of the couch, ignoring the phone, and rubs his face in his hands. Breathing hard, he says, "I'm sorry, Sidney, but I can't do this."

Something inside me shatters when he says it. I don't understand what's happening. Instead of explaining, Peter stands and turns away from me. I can't see his face. His bare back faces me with every muscle tense. Peter puts his hands on top of his head and sighs loudly, looking up at the ceiling before turning back to me. My heart stops when he looks at me. If I thought he was hot before, he is so much hotter now. Every curve of his chest is chiseled like a piece of art. But those eyes, those haunted blue eyes, make me transfixed. I stare at him, not knowing what he's thinking or why.

The phone stops ringing. The silence is thick. It floods the apartment in a wave. I can't breathe. Peter picks up his shirt and slips it back on. As he does that, I fix my bra strap and my dress, concealing myself.

I feel so hot, and so nervous. I want to know why he pushed me away. I've never had a guy do this before. I feel foolish to have done so much with him and then have him react like this. I wonder if I did something wrong. I glance at his back. He's standing across from me, out of arm's reach. "I'm sorry, Peter. I didn't think things would go that way. I really came up here to talk to you."

I mean every word I say. I had no intention of sleeping with him, but once his lips were on me, I wanted to feel something for a while, something besides the normal unending pain and remorse that flows through my veins. It would have been a moment to lose myself and forget everything, a chance to move on.

I'm greedy. I took too much. I should have said no. I should have responded like a normal girl and been shy about it. The thing is, I'm not normal. Too many things have happened. Knots twist me up inside. I can't look at him.

Peter's eyes search my face. I feel his gaze on me but I don't look up. Shoving his hands into his pockets, Peter's gaze falls to the floor. "I know. Coffee..." It seems as though he's going to say more, but he doesn't. Peter glances up at me from under his brow for a second.

My stomach sinks into my shoes. Panic, guilt, and fury are mixing together, making me feel sick. Peter doesn't look up. He doesn't say anything else.

The silence between us is clanging furiously. I have to leave. Every part of me wants to run. Humiliation doesn't look good on me. I try to smile, but it feels wrong. My jaw is stiff.

I can't think of anything else to tell him—anything to make it better—so I grab my purse and say, "Thanks for the sandwich." The last word comes out dripping with innuendo that I didn't mean. My voice caught in my throat at the wrong time. Horrified, I look up at him.

A bashful look slips across Peter's face. *Oh my god.* I didn't see it before, but he's shy. There's a trace of a wary boy left in this man. I think I may die. He's perfect. He's perfect and he's pushing me away.

Peter regains his confident composure and locks the shy part away. He leans in and kisses my cheek. "Thanks for everything."

We say a few other things, but the feeling to hold onto him doesn't subside. It's hard to leave. I feel as though I hurt him somehow, but I can't stay. Not after this. It's not the kind of thing I can recover from. And if I see him again, we won't be friends. There won't be a second chance after this. He's seen too much of me, and his tossing my ass out isn't something I want to repeat. I follow Peter to the door. He doesn't say anything else. I turn toward him, look up at his face with my lips parted. My question is all over my face even though I don't ask.

Peter's gaze cuts to the side. Fine. He won't even look at me. Whatever. I resist the urge to chew him out and stomp down the stairs like a mad elephant. Peter walks out and stands on the landing until I'm safe inside my car. I drive away without looking back.

CHAPTER 4

When I get back to the dorm room, I'm in a foul mood. I met the perfect man and screwed it up. I don't even know what I did! Was it raking my nails on his arm? Did I remind him of his dead cat or something? I walk down the hallway. The doors are all open. I live in an all-girls dorm. Some are in their PJs while others are still wearing their clothes from the day.

I pass a few doors and wave to the girls inside. Someone whistles at me as I walk by. "Hot mama!" a blonde girl shouts. I don't know her very well. We wave coming and going to class every day and that's about it.

I look at her and she waggles her eyebrows at me, assuming that I got some.

Yeah, I got nothing.

I round the corner and see my door open at the end of the hall. Dread fills my throat with worry. I don't want to discuss Peter with Millie. Plus, she's going to be pissed that I ditched her at dinner. That was a crappy thing to do, but Dusty—oh my God. Could she possibly pick someone more inappropriate? The only thing worse would have been a grizzly old biker with a toe fetish. Damn.

I stare at the door and feel the decision wash through me. What happened with Peter is best forgotten. I don't want to talk about it. Getting rejected is bad enough, but the fact that I just met him and let him do so much, and then got rejected—well, that's worse. It's like rejection a la mode. As if regular blow offs weren't cool enough. I shake out my worries and try to put on my game face. Nothing's wrong.

Our room is the social hub of the floor tonight. I walk inside and step over six girls doing crunches on the floor. I look at Millie and give her a what-the-fuck face.

DAMAGED

She's sitting on her chair by our shared desk. It's built into the wall. From the lack of sweat and general lack of agony, I assume that she's waiting her turn. There's no more room on the floor. "We found an old Abs of Steel tape. Megan said she could do the entire workout. We all took bets on who's going to die first."

I nod and sit down on my bed, tossing my purse on the nightstand. Millie watches me for a second. I can tell she wants to talk, but she won't say anything, yet. Good. I kick off my heels and grab my stuff and head to the showers.

Today sucked. I want to wash it all away. The entire day.

As I stand in the shower, I let the hot water blast me, but no matter how long I stand there, I can't get the memory of Peter's hands on my body to go away. It's as if he tattooed his touch on my mind. I don't know what I did wrong. I don't know if I would have had sex with Peter tonight—going that far, that fast would have been unusual for me—but I didn't think things would have ended so abruptly, either.

I try to shake off the hot and bothered feeling that has me coiled so tight, and head back to my room. It's been about twenty minutes since I left. Six girls are lying on the floor, clutching their stomachs.

"Oh my god! I'm gonna die." Evie says, from her side. She's curled into a ball. Her dark hair spills around her head on the floor like a bottle of ink.

"I told ya'll that it was hard! I told you, but no one ever listens to me!" Millie's talking with her hands on her hips, giving everyone an I told you so.

"So," I interrupt, "who won?"

Mille looks at the sorry lot and shakes her head. "Tia lasted the longest. Nine minutes."

Tia raises her arm in the air and sticks up her thumb.

I laugh, "Awesome, Tia, and congrats to all of you. That workout is insane. You're all going to be hunched over like 90-year-olds tomorrow."

Someone starts to laugh, but it's quickly followed by a moan of remorse.

Millie looks up at me from her bed. She's sitting with her legs folded, hands in her lap. "So, where'd you disappear to all night? I thought you would've wanted in on this?" Millie has a head of soft blonde curls. She pulled them up into a high ponytail when she got home and is wearing a tank and boxers.

I shrug as if it doesn't matter, but the pressure inside my chest tells me that it does. "Nowhere, really. I'm sorry I bailed on you."

Millie seems annoyed, but then her shoulders slump and I can tell she's forgiven me. "I shouldn't have made you come."

Tia blurts out, "You took her on another blind date? You must want your ass kicked, Millie." It's true. Everyone else knows better than to ask me by this point in the year.

"Jersey Girl won't kick my butt," Millie says, and makes a face at Tia. "I've got immunity."

I laugh, "Not after tonight. No more blind dates. Please restrain yourself and don't set me up with anymore assholes, okay? I can find them all by myself and when I do, I need you to feed me ice cream until I puke."

"Ice cream?" Tia says from the floor. I glance down at her in time to see her sit up. Her face contorts in pain. "What are you, twelve? Big girls get hammered after a shitty date."

I don't get hammered. Not anymore, but none of them know that. I laugh with them and agree to go to the bar tomorrow night. I have to work the following morning, so I can skip out early—*un*hammered—and no one will think anything of it.

———

The next morning I arrive at work early. I'm a teacher's assistant, a TA. I work in the English department, since that's my major. The offices are upstairs, away from all the classrooms. Me and a few other student workers are milling about, wondering where the professors are since the offices are glaringly empty. At this time of day, the place is usually bustling with activity, phones ringing and copy machines humming. The profs are usually in a rush to make it to their 8:00am classes, but today isn't like that.

Today it's eerily silent.

I walk in and head back to Tadwick's office. There's no indication that he's here; no steaming coffee mug, no glowing computer screen. He must be running late.

I put my purse in his desk drawer so no one swipes it, and look at the pictures on his desk. Tadwick's not that old for a professor, maybe forty-five, with thick brown hair and dark eyes. There are two little girls in one frame looking at Tadwick like he's the world's best dad. They seem happy, which is so different from my home life, I can't even imagine it.

I walk back out of his office and join the others. Someone calls 'five minute rule' and we all laugh. I hop onto an empty student worker desk that's located outside of Dr. Tadwick's office. The Graduate Assistant or GA, Marshal, is pacing, wearing a hole in the carpet. Being late is something he can't fathom. Add that to his slightly OCD personality and he looks like a caged lunatic. We're all going to be late, because something is obviously going on, so it's not as if this tardy will be his fault. Classes have already begun. It's 8:05am. All the TA's and GA's are supposed to sign in and then head to class, but no one is in the main office. The sign in sheet isn't out. Nothing's out. Everything is still locked up like it's the middle of the night.

All the teachers are gathered in a conference room at the end of the hall. One of the student's, Ryan, tried standing outside the door to listen, but eventually he came back saying that he couldn't hear a thing.

"Where is everyone?" Marshal asks me in a panicky voice. He's a tall skinny blonde with a skater's body; meaning lots of tightly corded muscle, not too big, not too small. He's easy on the eyes. Unfortunately, he's way too crazy to consider. Take a high-maintenance girl that's a total control freak and socially oblivious, and that pretty much sums up Marshal's personality. Even though he's a bit hard to put up with, the teachers love him because of his impeccable work. Everything he does is perfect.

"They're in the conference room," I say, picking at my nail. An uneasy feeling is swimming in my gut. I can't imagine what would make them blow off the workers and their classes this way.

Marshal huffs, "Discussing what? Class already started. You know all the 101 classes are going to call five minutes and leave."

I nod. "True, but Tadwick's harsh. He's shown up twenty minutes late before and marked everyone absent." Since he only allows two misses, that screwed over half of the class. "The man's a legend, in terms of avoiding his wrath, anyway. I doubt they'll leave."

Marshal and I are assigned to the same professor. He takes care of the upper-level classes and I do the 101 classes. Since the sound of my nervous nail picking is making Marshal glare at me, I switch and rub at a piece of lint on my sweater. He sighs and shakes his head. It's not my fault that I respond to tension by fidgeting. Besides, I didn't sleep too good last night, and I refuse to have two craptacular days in a row.

I fixed a smile on my face this morning, and it's not leaving my face, no matter what happens.

I swing my legs and lean forward on the desk, planting a hand on either side of my hips. A second later, Tia staggers in and flops onto a couch on the other side of the room. All of her things fall on the floor next to her and she moans.

"What's wrong with her?" Marshal asks, glancing back at Tia. "I hope she's not sick. She can't be here if she's sick." His voice raises half an octave as he speaks.

"Calm down, lunatic. She won the Abs of Steel workout last night." He blinks at me, not understanding.

Tia interjects, "My abs weren't up to it. Fucking Pilates class. It feels like someone used my guts for a punching bag." She groans and rolls onto her side.

Suddenly, Marshal turns toward me. "I think that story about Tadwick failing half the class is just a rumor." He taps his fingers to his lips and says, "But still, a good rumor has been known to strike fear into freshmen. Maybe they'll stay."

"They'll stay," Tia says, from across the room. I don't why she laid down. She won't be able to sit back up. Tia's hand waves in the air as she speaks. "My class, on the other hand, is probably already gone. They don't wait two seconds for Strictland."

Marshal glances at her and waves her off. "That's because Strictland's a pushover."

Someone clears her throat from the doorway behind Marshal. "Am I? I wasn't aware of that." Dr. Strictland walks into the center of the room. It's the central space between all the offices. She glances at Marshal. "I'll go harder on the class this semester and tell them to thank you for it, Marshal."

Marshal's eyeballs are going to pop out of his head. The corner of Strictland's mouth tugs up. She likes teasing him. Marshal has an issue with understanding sarcasm. Strictland gives him a look and says, "As if I'd do such a thing? Really Marshal. Learn to tell when someone is pulling your leg."

Dr. Cyianna Strictland is the head of the department. She's an older woman, with copper-colored skin and streaks of gray peppered through her auburn hair. She usually wears a vivid pant suit, but today she's wearing solid black, which is very out of character. Strictland waves her hand to cut off Marshal's groveling pleas. The look in her eye makes my stomach drop. Something bad has happened.

Continuing, Strictland folds her hands in front of her and says, "There are more important things to discuss. I'm afraid that I have some bad news. As you may know, Dr. Tadwick's classes have been twice a week since last year when he had a heart attack. He made a stunning recovery and was about to start back full time, however—" she presses her palms together and looks around the room at us, "Things didn't go as planned. Dr. Tadwick passed away over the weekend."

My jaw drops open along with everyone else's. Tadwick joked about his heart attack when he came back to work. He was so full of life, so young compared to the other profs. He had a new outlook on life and was ready to make a dent in the world. Most of the professors here could pass for twice his age. In comparison, Tadwick's the young teacher. He was the teacher everyone hoped to get.

Shocked gasps fill the room. I see my horror mirrored in the faces around me. We all liked him. Strictland gives us a moment and then speaks gently, "I know, I know. It was sudden. Everyone thought he would…" Strictland's voice is strained. She tries to keep the emotion off her face, but she can't. "He was a trusted colleague and a good friend.

"In light of what happened, we have had to find a quick replacement so that the students in Dr. Tadwick's classes could complete their courses. The university has hired a new teacher, one of my previous students, to temporarily to teach his classes.

"Sidney and Marshal, you can meet him in a moment. He's gone to the classroom to inform the students of the change. I'm not certain if he plans to hold class today or let the students leave. We left that decision up to him." Marshal and I nod.

I can't believe Tadwick's dead. A wave of shock hits me and doesn't let go. *His poor little girls.* My heart clenches inside my chest. I met them a few times. The last time I saw them, they came up here with their mother to bring Tadwick dinner. It was a big surprise. Now he's gone. There'll be a hole in that family that won't mend. My eyes sting, but tears don't fall. I've spent too much of my life crying. They won't fall unless I let them, and I can't. Not here. Not now.

Strictland eyes me, as though she can see my thoughts on my face. "The funeral is this afternoon, if you would like to attend and pay your respects." Strictland gives the location along with some other directions before turning to me and saying, "Please help the classes transition. Some of the students may be very upset. Dr. Tadwick was a promising young teacher. No one expected this."

I know the students will be upset, especially in Marshal's classes. The upper-level classes are small. Everyone knows everyone else. My 100 level classes are large with hundreds of students. Most of them didn't know Tadwick very well. I have no idea how they'll take it. Stunned, I nod and turn to leave. My class is downstairs right now and the new guy is probably being eaten alive.

I feel that hollow place at the center of my chest as I walk down the stairs and think about Tadwick. My emotions are such a jumbled mess. Add in the incident from last night and I can feel my grip on my emotions slipping away. I keep getting blindsided. Images flash through my mind, filled with Tadwick's smile, his voice, his lessons—things he taught me that won't ever be forgotten. For the vibrancy of his life to be snuffed out, it just seems so pointless. It's not fair. I feel the weight inside my chest sink into my stomach and think I might puke. I can't do anything except think that Tadwick's still alive, wearing his patchwork coat with the big ugly buttons. I picture him at the lectern, and know that I won't see him there ever again.

There are some people who take the time to teach others. And, at the time, it seems silly. At the time, I thought I knew everything, but Tadwick had a gentle way about him. *Life is a journey*, he would say. *No one knows everything, and the best part is that you don't have to.* He meant that I didn't have to figure everything out to live my life.

There's a difference between wisdom and knowledge. Tadwick was wise. My throat is in knots as I approach the classroom door. Normally, I would enter from the side and go sit in the first row, but not today.

The lump in my throat has grown so large, so impossible to swallow. I stand in front of the main doors to the classroom, and stare at the silver pulls without moving. I say a little prayer for Tadwick, inside my head, for his family, before I go inside. I don't really believe anything, but I can't help it. It seems like the right thing to do.

When I pull open the classroom door, I see the endless rows of seats. They are still full. I guess new guy is continuing class without a break. A student is talking, answering a question from *Antigone*, the assignment for today.

Glancing down to the front of the room, I see the new teacher's black suit and don't bother to look at his face. I walk down the stairs slowly. No one looks at me. They all know I'm the TA. I stare at my feet as I walk down the staircase toward the front of the massive room. I feel as if I'm in a bubble. The sounds around me blur, but about half way down the stairs my attention snaps to the front of the room. The hairs on my neck prickle and I feel eyes on me.

Slowly I lift my gaze to see who's looking at me. They lock on the man at the front of the room. He stares at me for a moment, and I shudder. Every inch of my body is in overload. I feel my brain breaking and falling apart inside my head.

This can't be happening, not to me, not now.

I stop and stare.

It's Peter.

CHAPTER 5

Every inch of my skin is covered in goose bumps. A shiver of ice runs down my spine and mingles with the lust still brimming inside of me from last night. Standing frozen on the stairs, I gape at him. Peter looks up at me with those gorgeous eyes. His mouth is paused midsentence as he stares back with his head titled to the side. Peter blinks at me, as if I'll fade away—like this is a bad dream and a single blink will set me free.

I have no idea what he's thinking. The expression on his face is so annoyingly neutral. Horror slowly drips through me like acid, burning away every other emotion. Although I can't feel them at the moment, I know they are still there, pushed back behind the floodgate that's ready to burst open.

Realization comes to me as I take in his clothing –that polished suit that fits his beautiful body perfectly. He's standing in front of the lectern. He is (or was) answering the student. *Awh, damn.*

Peter's the replacement professor.

Peter's a teacher.

Peter's my boss.

My heart feels brittle, like glass, like I'll shatter if I breathe. There's too much pressure even though nothing is touching me. I feel its force crushing against my body, against my battered soul. Too many things have gone wrong today. I feel the fracture lines splinter me into pieces.

I react. I don't mean to, but I do. Gasping, I cover my mouth and press my lips together so tightly that they hurt. Part of my mind is telling my legs to move, be quiet, and go sit down, but I can't. I'm frozen on the stairs and falling apart. Peter watches me with those striking eyes. He doesn't look away from me. He stands frozen, as if I'm the biggest shock he could have expected.

The student who was talking before, Lily, speaks up. I see her hand go up out of the corner of my eye. She asks, "Excuse me, Dr. Granz?"

Peter flinches and his head turns back toward Lily. There's a full smile on his face, as if nothing's happened. Like I don't matter. The students around me glance at my frozen form, still standing on the stair case. Peter's rich voice fills the room. It echoes through the speaker so clearly that I can't stand it. My legs are telling me to haul ass out of there, but I can't.

I drop my hand from my face and walk down to my normal seat at the front of the room. Peter doesn't look at me again. The rest of the class continues and I do my job, taking attendance and posting his questions to the interactive computer thingy the school purchased last year. The students use an iTouch to respond, and the teacher can see their answers. It helps the teacher and the students, but most of the teachers can't use it, which is why each class has a TA or GA to help.

Over the course of the hour, I've gone numb. I can't handle this. Too much has happened too fast. It's bad enough being here, in Tadwick's room, knowing I'll never see him again. Add to that the Peter complication and I can't do it. I can't handle seeing him every day, having him tell me what to do, sitting with him for hours and grading papers. My stomach twists and turns, growing more acidic by the second. I feel so sick. By the end of class, I've shrunk back into my chair so that my head barely hits the top of the seat.

Peter dismisses the class. He turns and looks at the lectern for a moment, while I gather my things to leave. As I stand and start walking up the stairs, I hear my name. "Sidney Colleli, please come see me before you go." I hear the rustling of paper behind me as Peter picks up his notes.

Turning slowly, I look back at him. The lump in my throat is now the size of my head. I can't swallow. I'm coming apart at the seams. I can feel it. Talking to him is a very bad idea, but there are a few students lingering. I can't blow him off.

As it is, people noticed something was weird when I saw Peter. Dating a prof is against university policy, so is dating the boss. Peter is both. We'll both get fired if anyone knows what happened between us. There is no room for stuff of this sort in academia. The rules were made crystal clear when we signed on the line to be a TA. At the time, the thought of sleeping with a prof sounded gross, but now—*shit, shit, shit.* My brain is in panic mode. I try to lock it down as I walk toward Peter.

I grin at him, as if he has no effect on me, and fold my arms over my chest. "So, *Doctor* Granz, is it?"

Peter looks at me from under his brow. He stacks papers and shoves them into his satchel. "Yes, I completed my doctoral work last semester. The title is new. It takes some getting used to."

I nod. "Mmm, I suppose that's why you forgot to mention it."

Peter gives me a look that says I shouldn't be talking about this now. His eyes burn a hole into mine, like he's daring me to blurt it out. I break the death-stare first and look away. I don't have it in me right now. Peter clears his throat and says, "Please meet me in my office at 3:00pm. There are some things we need to go over right away." He grabs another stack of papers from his bag as he speaks. He pulls them out and puts them on the podium.

I don't answer him at first. I just look at my shoes, my tired old All Stars. Then, my gaze drifts to his black dress shoe. It's a saddle shoe, vintage, and one of my favorite styles. It reminds me of dancing and laughing, things that seem so foreign at the moment.

I open my mouth as if I'm going to say something and decide that it's not worth it. I need this job. I worked my ass off to get here and I'm not letting Peter mess it up. I nod and turn away. I don't look back at him. I walk up the stairs.

A plan forms in my head. I need to put space between us. I need to get a different professor to work for. I need to find Strictland and ask her to assign me to someone else.

As I reach the upper landing, I see Marshal walk through the door. He gives me a look and tilts his head at Peter. "So, how is he?"

I glance back, watching him write on the dry-erase board with his back to me. When I turn to Marshal, I snap, "Why would I know?"

Marshal gives me a weird look. I push past him, banging into his shoulder because he doesn't move and I don't want to stay around to chat.

I need to find Strictland. Now.

———

When I reach the offices, things appear to be back to normal. Student workers are at their desks, professors are hurrying through the space—coffee in one hand, papers in the other—on their way to teach.

I walk over to Tadwick's office and stand in the open door way. I spent hours in there. Leaning my head to the side, I rest it against the doorjamb. My eyes scan the room looking at all Tadwick's books, his favorite poems and literature. My gaze drifts to his pictures and some small clay thing that looks like a squashed cat. One of his girls made that for him. I remember him bringing it in and proudly showing off his future artist. He was beaming that day.

Blinking rapidly, I try to fight off the stinging that's building behind my eyes. Life is short. I know that, but I can't believe he's gone. I can't believe I won't see him again. It feels unreal. My mind wrestles with it and doesn't want to accept that it's a fact—Dr. Tadwick is dead.

A hand lands on my shoulder and I nearly jump out of my skin. I round on the person swiftly, trying hard not to punch the crazy person. Sneaking up on me is normally a bad idea, but today, it's a super bad idea. I'm angry. I'm shocked. I'm a million things and nothing. I want to hit something. The pain that would shoot through my hand would make it so I'd feel something familiar, something I know how to handle.

I don't know how to handle this.

Before I smash in her face, I see Dr. Strictland. She doesn't step back or lower her hand when I turn. She has that smile on her face, the one that isn't really a smile. It's a way to hide pain, a mask. "Are you all right, Sidney? I know you and Marshal must be in shock as well."

"I'm okay," I say, trying to force my voice to sound normal.

That's my go-to response. *I'm fine. I'm okay. Everything's great.* But nothing's great. Everything sucks. My fake smile slips from my face. "Okay, I'm lying. I'm not okay. I didn't expect this. I'm not sure what to do."

Strictland looks at me with such compassion that it's hard to maintain her gaze and not cry. "Come with me." Lowering her hand, she turns away, and I follow her back to her office.

When I was first in here, I thought she was a deranged cat lady. There are kitty cat statues and pictures everywhere, and I mean everywhere. Little plastic kittens hang playfully from the lights, ceramic orange cats sit on her shelves, there are cross-stitched kitties on the chairs, and on her desk cat frames surround more pictures of real housecats. Seriously. It's scary. Eventually, I found out that she had been the victim of a prank and left the cat theme in place when she realized it scared the crap out of people. She has an interesting sense of humor.

I lower myself onto a stitched kitty and lean back into the chair. Strictland walks behind her desk and sits down. "Sidney, I know today was hard for you. Have you lost anyone before, dear?"

I nod and keep my hands folded tightly in my lap. "Yes."

She nods slowly, waiting for me to elaborate, but I don't. There are things I won't say, secrets I won't tell. I can't talk about it. Not now, not ever. "Well, you can talk to a counselor about it and work through the stages of grief. It's better that you're not alone in this. We're all going to miss him." I nod. "How was the freshmen class this morning?"

I glance up at her. "They were all right. Dr. Granz continued with the lesson." I pause and decide to just blurt it out. "Is there any way that I could get transferred to another professor?"

Strictland looks surprised. She leans forward and places her hands on top of her desk. "Why? Is something wrong? Did Dr. Granz—"

"No," I say, quickly backtracking. "It's just that I don't think that I can manage to sit in Tadwick's office every day. It'd be so much better if I could work for someone else." I'm lying. Sort of. I don't want to sit there with Peter every day. I don't want to look up at him and remember his hands on me, and I sure as hell don't want to remember him throwing me out.

Dr. Tadwick shakes her head. "I'm sorry, Sidney, but all the TA jobs have been assigned for months now. There are no other positions. You'll have to figure out how to deal with this loss, and I'm sure Dr. Granz will be happy to help you, unless you're resigning?" Her eyes widen as she looks at me. The last thing she wants to do is hire and train a new TA in the middle of the year.

"No, I'm not resigning. I need this job." I look at my hands, at the way the nail polish that was so neat last night has been chipped away. Images from the previous evening flash across my mind. I see Peter's eyes and hear his voice echo inside my head. The sensation of his hands searing my skin and his teasing kiss rushes back. I press my lips together and shut the memory out. I'm going to have to suck it up. Peter is a part of my life now, whether I want him there or not.

CHAPTER 6

I'm a nervous wreck by the time I get to lunch. Before finding my regular table with Millie and Tia, I walk into the cafeteria and grab some food. I navigate my way through hordes of students, and sit down next to Millie at a long table in front of the windows. This entire side of the cafeteria is windows. The school sunk a buttload of money into the view. There's a lot of brick work, flowers, and super green grass. Seriously, it's too green. I thought it was plastic at first. Everything around here is that sickly shade of yellow that comes from a general lack of water. There's been a drought here for the past three years, and it's easy to tell. That's why this little garden stands out. It's completely out of place, but it looks good when prospective students sit down.

When I sit down, Millie's picking at a salad as though one piece of lettuce might be tastier than another. There's no dressing on it. She eats it dry. My plate has a corndog and fries. Bad days call for foods that are bad for your butt. I dip my dog into ketchup and take a bite. I'm not that hungry, but maybe eating something will help me feel better.

Tia looks at me like I'm eating asphalt off the road with a side of squirrel. I snap, "What?"

"Nothing," Tia responds, glancing down at her own plate.

Millie sighs and glances at me. "What's wrong? You seem off-balance." She stabs another piece of salad and turns the leaf over, examining it, before popping it in her mouth.

"Nothing." *Everything.* "Today is just turning into crap, that's all." My favorite teacher died. I nearly slept with a guy last night, but he blew me off. Oh, and he's my new boss. What a train wreck.

Tia choses that moment to say, "I heard Tadwick's replacement already called you into his office. What'd you do?"

"Way to be tactless, Tia." Millie scolds, shaking her head and spearing more greens onto her fork.

"Who told you that?" I ask, not caring that Tia's blunt.

"Marshal. He was in a mood after class. He said something about how you pissed off Dr. Grant—"

"Granz," I correct.

"Yeah, him, and how you pissed him off already. Seriously, Sidney, what'd you do?" Tia leans forward. She's sitting across from me and hasn't touched her food.

I shrug and paint my plate red with the half eaten corndog. Ketchup streaks across the white dish in wide arcs while I tell them, "I don't know. Granz just seems mean. He probably wants to make a point with me or something stupid like that. You know how teachers are hard-asses on their first day." That's usually true. It sets the tone for the rest of the year. A professor who's a pushover on day one, is a doormat on day two.

Millie's eyes have been burning a hole in the side of my face. "Well, in light of today sucking, I think we should end the night with some margaritas."

"You always want to end the night with margaritas," I respond, still not looking at her. My ketchup resembles a disturbing Van Gogh painting. I could call it, *The Missing Ear.*

"Well, you've needed one lately. Take a hint already." Millie's back straightens and she looks straight ahead. Tia ducks her head and eats her food, not looking at either of us.

"Take a hint? What are you talking about?" Millie says nothing. She just looks at me like I should know, but I don't get it. "Come on Millie, if you've got something to say, say it." I've dropped my corndog, sensing a verbal bitch-slap coming on.

She looks as thought she's going to say something and then thinks better of it. Instead, Millie shakes her head and says, "It's nothing."

"No, come on—tell me."

"I really shouldn't—"

"Just say it!"

"Fine!" she shouts way too loud for her little body. Blonde curls bouncing, she grips the table and yells, "Nothing makes you happy. Everything I do is wrong. Every guy is wrong. Everyone is wrong. Jeeze, Sidney! You ever stop to wonder if it's you? I mean, when that many things are wrong, maybe *you* are the one who's wrong? Maybe *you* are the one that doesn't fit."

I blink at her. This is as much of an argument as I've ever gotten from Millie. On another day, I could have brushed it off. On another day, I might have laughed and agreed with her—but not today.

I stand up and grab my tray. I walk away without speaking. Millie's words cut me to the core, because out of all the things that are wrong with me, that's the one that's been hanging around my neck like a noose. I don't fit anywhere. Maybe I pretend that's okay, but it's not. The isolation makes me crazy. I feel as if I've been drifting on a crappy little blow-up boat, and my best friend just popped it.

Millie's voice rings out behind me, but I don't stop. I dump my tray with my half-eaten food and leave. Pushing through the doors to the campus center, I step outside into the warm afternoon air. I walk fast and hard, not thinking about where I'm going. I just go.

When I stop, I'm standing at the bottom of a grand staircase at the front of the oldest building on campus. No one uses the stairs. There are too many of them. Everyone enters the building through the back and takes the elevator. I climb the steps until I'm close to the top and sit at the foot of a massive pillar. I pull my knees into my chest and wrap my arms around them.

There are no words sometimes. There's nothing to say to make things better.

There's an hour to kill before class. Then, I have to haul myself back to the English building and face Peter. I lower my forehead to my knees.

Why do bad things always seem to happen in threes? Is there some cosmic law that I don't know about? First Peter, then Tadwick, and then what? There'll be a third thing, probably my job. Peter will most likely want to replace me with someone that he hasn't seen half-naked. My mind wanders. I think about his eyes, his face. I can't believe Peter has a doctorate. He doesn't look much older than me, but I guess he is.

My life is a mess. Whoever said college was easier than real life doesn't know crap.

Ever since I left New Jersey, things have been hard. It seems that I ran away from one problem and straight into another. Nothing's gone right for me. I'm always in the wrong place at the wrong time. When God was dishing out luck, I didn't get any. Instead, I got a shitload of someone else's bad karma. Maybe I was a total ass in a past life and this life is payback. Too bad I don't believe in that stuff. At least that would make sense. The way things are now, nothing makes sense.

My family hates me. What I told Peter about them freaking out when I left, it was true, albeit a slightly subdued variation of the truth. They wanted me to stay and take a job at the bank. Family is everything. *Blood is thicker than water*, whatever that means. But, I had this chance and I took it. I applied at a school that had a scholarship within my reach. They gave it to me along with the TA job and I've been able to support myself. I never thought I'd be able to do that. I don't want to rely on anyone else. It hurts too badly when they let you down. I've fallen on my face enough times to know that there's no one else who will take care of me as well as I can.

Maybe I'm broken. Maybe I am wrong and Millie is right. I don't know. *You don't have to know everything.* I lift my head and look up, hearing Tadwick's advice inside my head, remembering his words. Some of the weight lifts from my shoulders. That's his legacy—all the students he taught—all the positive influences he left behind. That's his footprint. I wonder what mine will be.

CHAPTER 7

My stomach floods with dread as I walk toward the English building. I don't want to see Peter. I don't want to see his eyes. I don't want to hear him say whatever he's going to say. And I swear, if he makes up some lame excuse about last night, I'll lose it.

I manage to get to the offices and slowly move toward Tadwick's room. I wish I didn't care. I wish Peter didn't matter, but last night was so awesome and I thought we had something. I was wrong. I hate being wrong.

I drop my sociology books on the student desk since it's empty. The office door is closed. I step up and knock. My heart slaps into my ribs and my pulse shoots into dangerous territory. I wait, but no one answers. I knock again and feel the hairs on the back of my neck stand on end. A slow sinking feeling fills my stomach and I turn slowly.

Peter is behind me with a stern look on his face. "We're over here," he says, and walks away expecting me to follow. We cross the hall and enter a different office. This one is barren. There are no books, cats, or picture frames to be found. I step into the office, past Peter, and he pushes the door closed behind me. Peter gestures for me to take a seat. I sit down in one of the chairs in front of his empty desk. Peter walks around me and sits behind the desk.

His blue eyes search my face, but I stare at him blankly. I need to be numb. I tell myself, *No matter what he says, no matter what happens, don't react.*

"How are you?" he asks. I arch an eyebrow at him, like it's a stupid question. "That good, huh?"

I tap my teeth together once and glare at him. "Enough with the pleasantries, Dr.

Granz. I want to know if you intend on replacing me as your TA, or if we're going to lie to everyone and pretend we don't know each other." I'm as prickly like a withered rose, all thorns.

His jaw drops for a second. He leans forward, looking at me as though I shouldn't think poorly of him. "I didn't know you were a student. I thought you were older. You seemed older when you sat down."

"I didn't know you were a teacher." My eyes slip over his face, and then slip down to his tie and perfectly pressed white shirt before returning to his face. "I have trouble believing that you forgot you were a doctor. If you'd mentioned it, we could have avoided last night all together. I would have asked what you were a doctor of, and you would have told me. We both would have realized the problem and gone our separate ways."

"What's happened has happened. We can't change it—"

My temper is about to break free. I'm trying so hard not to yell. I point my index finger at him and say in a low voice, "Don't make me climb across this desk and slap you, because I will. Don't talk to me like I'm a child and tell me shit I already know. I asked a question. What are you going to do?"

Peter presses his fingertips together as I speak. Those blue eyes search my face, looking for something. After everything that's happened, I can't believe that he can still look me in the eye, or that he'd want to. He lets out a slow breath and drops his hands to the desk. "Nothing. I'm not going to do anything. Last night was an accident. I wasn't employed here yet and you weren't my student or employee, not yet."

"It's a technicality, and they won't care. If someone finds out and we don't say something now, you'll ruin your reputation and mine."

"So, you want tell Dr. Strictland?" He stands suddenly and walks to the door. "Let's go tell her." Peter's hand is on the knob, twisting it when I bounce out of my seat and block the door with my body.

"Don't you dare open that door." Peter towers above me and looks down into my face. He's too close, but I can't step out of the way. "You can't tell her. They'll fire me, not you."

"Then, what do you want me to do, Sidney?" Peter closes his eyes for a second and runs his fingers through his hair. It's the only indication he's given that this is stressing him out too. "I want to do what's right, but I don't want to hurt you more than I already have."

I stiffen. "You didn't hurt me," I lie. "And costing me my job isn't right."

Peter is silent. He steps away from the door. Our shoulders brush together as he turns away. It sends sparks through me, making my stomach twist. He doesn't seem to notice what he does to me. Peter sits behind the desk and leans back.

When I don't resume my place in the chair right away, he holds his palm out, indicating that I should sit. "Spell it out, Sidney. What do you want to do?"

My eyes dart between Peter and the floor. I don't want to lie to Strictland, but Peter's right. Technically we didn't do anything wrong, so there's nothing to tell. But it makes me uneasy. My world is turning into a house of cards. Throw another secret onto the pile. Sure. Why not?

"Nothing" I say. "We'll do nothing. Nothing happened. It wasn't important and it's not as though it'll happen again, so I don't think we need to say anything."

As I speak, Peter's eyes slip away from mine. He gazes at the bookcase behind me, looking through me like I'm not even there. "If that's what you think is best." I nod. He continues, "Very well..." Peter opens his mouth as if he's going to say something more, but he doesn't. I wish he would. I wish he'd tell me what I did wrong last night, what made him push me away. Can he tell that I'm fucked up? Can he tell that I've been torn to pieces and put back together again?

I don't let anyone get close to me. I keep them at arm's length. The walls guarding my heart went up a long time ago. They don't have cracks or crevices where someone can slip in. That's why I don't understand my reaction today. I shouldn't care. I would have left at the end of the night and never called. I don't want to know him, and I sure as hell don't want him to know me. But…there's a chink in my armor. There has to be.

I nod again, taking Peter's silence as a cue to leave. I stand and walk to the door. Peter doesn't get up. He watches me as I reach for the knob and says, "Sidney." I turn to look at him. "Be here early tomorrow."

"How early? For what?"

"Just do it, okay. Meet me here at 7:00am."

CHAPTER 8

The next morning I show up at Peter's office a few minutes early. I'm wearing a pair of jeans and a thick cream colored sweater. A steaming cup of coffee is in my hand. Trudging up the stairs to the second floor offices, I take a sip. The building is quiet this early. Hardly anyone is here. My pulse pounds harder with every step I take. I feel humiliated and it doesn't mesh well with my mood.

I'm going to act like Peter doesn't affect me. That's the plan. It's not stellar, but it's the best I can manage on short notice and scrambled brains. I tossed and turned all night. Sleep finally came around time to get up. Nights are hard enough. Add Peter the next morning, Tadwick's empty office, and I might cry for no apparent reason. Awesome.

I push through the double doors to the offices and see Marshal sitting inside. I breathe a sigh of relief. Thank God. I won't be alone with Peter.

Marshal looks at me. He's dressed like Bert from Sesame Street, with a striped shirt and turtleneck. He tops the look off with a pair of jeans and white sneakers. He looks like a six-year-old. "It's about time," he scolds me.

"It's not even 7:00 yet, you neurotic bundle of nerves. Chill out." I sip my coffee and set my book bag down on a table before settling into a chair. I lean back and relax. As long as Marshal is here, I can handle this. Confidence washes over me and my rapid pulse slows to normal. "Where is the geezer anyway?"

"Behind you," Peter says, walking by with his arms filled with papers and books. "Get up, Colleli, and bring Marshal with you." He backs into his office door and tries to get a key into the lock while balancing everything in his arms. It doesn't work. Papers start to slide and a book falls to the floor.

Marshal is oblivious. I wait for him to help with the door, but when he doesn't I get up and walk over to Peter. "I'll do it." I take the keys from his hand and our fingers brush. A jolt of electricity shots through me and swirls in my stomach. *Damn him.*

Peter backs away, apparently unaffected. "Thanks, Sidney."

I hold the door open and gesture for him to enter. Peter manages to get to his desk before everything falls out of his arms. Papers and books go everywhere. I kneel and start picking them up and putting them on his desk. "What is all this stuff?" They're the papers that were due a few weeks ago.

Marshal enters and stands there watching us with my coffee in one hand and my book bag in the other. "You forgot this."

"Thanks, Marshal." He sets my bag down inside the door and puts the cup on an empty shelf. Then, he stands there and watches us stooping, but doesn't help. Marshal just watches with his hands clutched in front of him. I glance up at him. "You might want to help."

"Oh no, I think you've got it." Marshal steps over us and sits in Peter's chair.

Peter gives me a look that says, *Is he serious?*

"Choose your battles wisely is all I'm going to say. If he wasn't an asset, they wouldn't have given him the job." Peter's eyes meet mine and he nods. He holds my gaze a beat too long, and I glance away.

We finally get everything picked up and onto the table when Peter tells us what's going on. "When Tadwick died, he had papers in his office and at his house. His wife gave these to me last night so the students wouldn't have to redo them. There are research papers, tests, and all sorts of things here that need to be graded and returned. Dr. Tadwick did some of them, but he didn't get a chance to finish. We need to figure out which papers go with which class and grade them. Today."

"What?" Marshal whines. "Why is this so last minute?"

"Marshal," I warn, but he doesn't listen.

"No, it's not fair. Why should I spend my morning sorting this mess? I'm not the one who dropped it, besides, it's not a part of my job description." He folds his arms over his chest.

Peter doesn't react the way I expect him to. He walks over to Marshal, and turns the chair so that they face each other. Peter braces his arm on the back of the chair and lowers his face toward Marshal's. "Do you like your job? Do you want to keep it?"

"Yes, but—"

"Then do what I ask you to do. Take that stack to Tadwick's office and sort them. When you're done, take the graduate papers you find and grade them, then give them to me to look over. Understand?" Peter speaks in a low stern voice. I can tell this isn't optional. Hell, even Marshal can tell he is getting scolded.

Marshal's eyes dart to the floor and he says, "Yes sir."

Peter stands up and tosses a pile of papers in Marshal's lap. "Get going. The door is open." Marshal takes the papers and leaves without looking back. Peter glances at me before sitting in his chair. "Is he always like that? I thought he was just out of it yesterday."

A lopsided smile forms on my face. "Pretty much. They say he makes up for in brains what he lacks in tact."

"Who says that?"

"I don't know, his mother?" Peter smiles and shakes his head. I didn't mean to be nice to him. I want to be cold and distant, but for some reason I can't. I glance at the doorway, wondering how difficult it is for Marshal. "I'm sure Marshal was shaken up yesterday. He's acting a little more nuts than usual." I sit down and start sorting the papers. Most of the class wrote their course number somewhere, so it isn't too hard, just time consuming.

Peter watches me for a second and nods before starting on the next pile. "I thought that it would help everyone to have these back as soon as possible, in light of what's happened. It's good to move forward."

I nod, not saying anything. I wonder if that's what he thinks about us too. Don't look back.

We sit in silence, sorting and stacking. Peter glances up at me from time to time, but he doesn't say much. When the silence is deafeningly loud, I say, "Start talking or I'll go crazy."

Peter glances at me from the corner of his eye. "Talk about what?"

"Anything, just say something. You've been all tense and quiet since I saw you yesterday. I thought nothing happened. Let's act like it." I'm such a liar. I just want something else to think about because right now my mind is filled with Peter's hands, Peter's eyes, Peter's breath.

He stills and looks at me as I speak. I don't look up. I keep sorting. He clears his throat. "I didn't say nothing happened. I said we did nothing wrong." Peter goes back to his pile and moves the papers into the stacks on his desk.

"Same difference." I take a deep breath and decide to just say it. "Listen, I don't really get along with that many people and I enjoyed talking to you the other day. Talking isn't against university policy, is it?" I tease.

Peter gives me a hesitant smile. "No, it's not. Okay, tell me something about yourself. How'd you end up here?"

I pause. Damn it. Out of everything to ask, he asks that. I hedge. "College."

"I know that," he says, looking up at me. "I mean what made you chose this college? Why leave and come here. This town is a hell hole and the people are a little weird, in case you didn't notice." He smiles at me.

I keep working as I speak. I might as well tell him. It's not like it'll change anything. "I traded one hell for another, I guess. I wanted to get as far away from my family as possible. Something happened during my senior year. They blamed me. I thought they should have defended me." I feel my heart pounding in my chest as the memory rushes forward in my mind. A chill wraps around my throat and chokes me. I swallow hard, forcing the feeling away. "Anyway, I came here because the university offered me a way to pay for college by myself. I wanted to start over. So here I am."

Peter's quiet. It's not the normal why I went to college story. I don't care what he thinks of me; at least I don't want to. He finally asks, "Was it worth it? I mean, cutting everyone off. Did it fix things?"

I feel his eyes on my face. I don't look up. I can't meet his gaze. Why did I tell him this? This conversation feels too intimate to be having with him. I expected Peter to gloss over it, as if he stepped in something icky, but he didn't. I smile weakly, trying to hold my mask in place, trying to push away the memories that haunt me. "I'm not sure that it's something that can be fixed. There are things like that, ya know? They change you and you can't be who you were before. It doesn't matter if it's fixed or not."

Peter surprises me and says, "I know what you mean." He doesn't elaborate. His eyes have the same vacant stare from the other night, as though he's remembering something he wants to forget. He blinks and says, "I didn't see you at Dr. Tadwick's funeral yesterday."

"I didn't go."

"Obviously. What I meant was that I'm surprised you didn't go."

"I couldn't." I'm staring at the paper in my hands, not seeing the words on the page. I hold it too long. "I couldn't bear to see his kids. I'm weak." The thought of Tadwick's daughters gathered around his casket with tears in their eyes was too much. I feel like I'm coming apart at the seams most days as it is. That would have unraveled me completely.

"No, you're not." Peter puts another paper onto a pile.

Shaking my head, I say, "You don't even know me. How can you possibly say that?" I stare at him, daring him to answer.

Peter lifts his head and our gazes lock. It's like the other night. The feelings rush back. Something inside me stirs. My body responds to him as if I'm made for him. The hollow spot in my chest tingles and feels full. Something inside tugs me toward him and I can't escape. I lose myself in his eyes. The bookcases and papers fade from sight and the only thing that I can see is Peter. His beautiful pink lips part, like he's going to whisper something to me, but Marshal enters the room. Peter straightens and turns away from me.

Marshal is oblivious to relationship stuff. He never notices anything, otherwise it would worry me. He walks into the room and shoves two stacks of papers into the bookcase. "These are the two graduate classes that I teach. The rest are yours. I have to go get the other stacks. Be right back." Marshal turns and leaves, not realizing that he interrupted anything.

I glance at the clock. It's close to 8:00am. "I better get downstairs."

"Go ahead," Peter says, his voice too soft. "I'll meet you there in a few minutes."

I nod and grab my bag. I leave the room as quickly as possible. I don't look back at Peter, but I feel his eyes on me as I walk away. Thoughts tumble through my brain like they're falling down a flight of stairs. They just keep coming and I can't make them stop. There's no way I can deny how I feel about Peter, but there's no way in hell I'm ever going to say anything. Getting rejected once is enough for me.

I walk down to the classroom, and then turn on the computers and other technology that is needed for the lesson. Everything comes online and flares to life, except for the microphone at the podium. I tap it, but it's dead. Damn it. There's a wire that runs through the bottom of the wood and goes into a port in the floor. I lie on my side and try to tuck my head under the podium into the tiny space between the wood and the floor. I wiggle my head under and see the socket. Reaching underneath, I fish my hand through cobwebs and dust hoping to God that a mutant rat from the science lab doesn't suddenly appear and gnaw off my arm.

"You okay?" I hear Peter ask from above me. I didn't realize he was standing there.

I don't pull my head out to look at him. My fingers are so close to the wire. "I'm fine. The mic is out. I'm fixing the wire. One second." I'm at an award angle, but I manage to get my fingers on the plug and push it back into the socket. The speakers make a hideous, deafeningly loud noise, and I hear everyone in the room moan in response. When I wiggle back out, Peter is standing above me with his hands over his ears.

"Weenie," I say to him. I know he's too close to the mic to say anything back.

Peter offers his hand and pulls me up. I dust myself off, trying to ignore how much I like the feel of his hands. A nervous jolt of excitement fills my body. Peter's gaze rests on my figure as I walk back to my seat. I don't turn back. It's everything I can do to act as though I don't know and don't care that he's looking.

It's then that one of the guys in the first row starts clapping. He *woos!* and says, "Let's hear it for the techie TA!" He claps loudly and everyone follows his lead. A crooked grin forms on my lips as I lean forward and look at him like he's crazy. The guy holds his hands up and claps louder and gestures for me to stand. Shaking my head, I stand and bow, smiling as I wave to the class.

The guy—Mark—watches me until I sit down. I nod at him and he smiles back, beaming. He's a year younger than me, and relationships are usually so far from my mind that I never noticed him before. Between the two, I suppose it was difficult for him to catch my attention. Mark's grin is contagious. I lean back in my seat, smiling, and look up at the podium, when I see Peter's face. His eyes are hard and the usual easy-going smile isn't visible. The look slips away before I can blink. Mark didn't notice. Hell, I'm not sure if I noticed it. What the hell was that?

Peter starts his lesson, and by the end of it, everyone is back in the groove of things. I wonder how long it will take for them to transition from Dr. Tadwick to Peter. They have different styles of teaching. I know from not only sitting in here, but because Peter is the professor in my once a week night class. , The thought makes me feel all twisted inside. When I reign in my drifting mind, Peter is dismissing the class. I stand and gather my things.

Peter walks over to me. "Thanks for taking care of the microphone. You saved me from a very sore throat. Talking loud enough for the entire room to hear all day would have severely sucked."

"Well, that's what I'm here for, to save the world from suckage." I give him a half smile and start to walk toward the side door.

"Can you do 7:00am for one more day? After that, we should be caught up." Peter's eyes slip over my face as he asks, more gently this time than yesterday.

I nod, acting as though I don't care, acting like it's a job and nothing more. "Sure. See you then.

CHAPTER 9

Millie is sitting on her bed, sorting through photocopies of reference books from the library. She's been working on a term paper for the past few days. The abs of steel night was when she decided to take a break. You don't want to be around Millie when she takes a break.

"Hey," I say, walking in and sitting on the bed opposite her after my classes are done. Our room is decorated with the things Millie enjoys. Since she has more money than me, and I had no intention of decorating it, I let her. Everything is yellow and blue.

After our fallout the other day, I felt bad. I'm sure I was out of sorts. We patched things up later that night. My ego is still bruised, but I'm glad we're not fighting anymore. She's my best friend.

"Hey Sid," she says back, not bothering to look up. Her fingers are racing across the paper, her eyes scanning the information. The bitch has a photographic memory. I'm super jealous. When she finishes, she looks up at me and smiles.

It feels like I fell off a cliff. "I know that look. What'd you do?" I ask her, as I yank my shoes off my feet.

"Nothing devious. Damn, Sidney. Can't a girl do something nice and smile about it?"

"Maybe, but your little brain doesn't work that way. Besides, I've seen that look enough times to know to run the other way when you give it to me, so let me make this easy on you. Whatever you did—whatever you were going to ask—the answer is no. Hell no. No way." I flop back on my bed and stare at the ceiling.

Today was long. The 7:00am start makes it feel later than it is. I still have homework and need to grab dinner. It's already getting late.

"But, Sidney, you didn't even hear what it is. I know you'll love it."

"You always say that."

"And you always love it."

"No, I don't. I'm just being polite."

Millie snort laughs, because that's a big fat lie. Polite comments and bluntness are two qualities that cannot coexist. I favor blunt. She knows. "As if that were possible." She throws her head back and makes a whiny sound. "Please, please, please, please…"

I glance at her. "Are you serious?" Millie clasps her hands together under her chin and is still chanting please, please, please. "Are you going to stop?" She shakes her head and continues pleading. "At least tell me what it is."

"Swing dance club. Please, please, please, please, please…" and she keeps on begging me and batting her huge eyes. Maybe that works on Brent, but I could care less.

"No," I say, and pull my arm over my face. She doesn't stop. I laugh at her and say, "Are you going to keep doing that?"

"Yes. Please, please, please…"

I love dancing, especially swing dancing. Between the music, the clothes, and the movement, I love it. There are few things that I can lose myself in. While I don't get modern club dances, which look like people spasming, I do enjoy the old dances. There are moves, steps, and rhythms to get lost in. It takes skill, and when you find the right partner, it's close to perfect. I haven't danced in a long time, not since I left New Jersey.

Millie is still pleading. I let her whine for a few more minutes and then cave. "Fine, but you owe me."

"You always say that."

"Yeah, well, you owe me a ton." She laughs and bounces up and down on her bed. "Where the hell did you find a swing dance club down here? I thought just about everything was country."

Millie's eyes slowly drift to the side. I sit up and prop myself onto my elbows and stare her down. She explains, "It's not that kind of club."

"What do you mean?"

"It's a club the school started. The student organization was trying to get it going last year, before the holidays, but we couldn't get a teacher to sponsor us. Well, they finally found someone. And it starts tonight!" She claps her hands like she's three and beams at me.

Oh my God, this is going to be lame. "A school club?" She nods. "Like chess team?"

"Like the awesome new swing dance club!" Millie is obviously excited.

I'm sorry that I said yes. A class full of newbs means I won't get to dance much. We'll be lucky to get past the basics.

Millie jumps up and runs across the room. "I found this dress at the mall. I can't believe it." She grabs a red dress from her closet and pulls it out. The bodice is fitted and it has a full circle skirt. It is perfect. "Now, I have to find saddle shoes!"

"T-straps would look cool with that too." I can't help it. I'm drooling. Millie hands me the dress, so I can admire it.

Awh, crap. She's sucking me in and I'm letting her. I glance up at her. "You're evil, you know that right?"

Millie beams at me and nods, "You're not going to regret this, Sidney. It's going to be so much fun!"

CHAPTER 10

Millie is wearing her new dress with a pair of heels. I'm wearing a black skirt and white blouse. It's boring, but it's the only thing I have that even comes close to swing clothes. The silky fabric swishes next to my thighs as we walk. The club was given use of the old gym. Old is literal. The gymnasium was constructed in 1919. It has no air conditioning, which is an issue in the heat. But Swing Dance Club is pretty low on the roster, in terms of getting a good room to use, so we were banished to sweat it out in the oldest building on campus. The façade is all brick and the inside smells of moldy socks.

Millie pulls open the door, and we walk through the darkened halls and find the gym. It's much smaller than the new one. We go inside and see Brent. Millie runs over to him and throws her arms around his neck. He holds her tightly and spins her around. Her red skirt twirls as he does it and Millie laughs. I smile at them. She seems happy, which makes me happy. Despite Millie's shortcomings, she's a good friend.

I walk over when Brent puts her down. The club isn't very big. There are less than a dozen kids standing around. From the looks of it, most of them are girls that like the idea of dressing up and dancing. The guys tagged along hoping to get lucky for being such good sports. Guys can be so dumb. Dancing, especially this kind of dancing, is a chance to get close to a girl. He can feel her whole body against his and it's expected. Dancing is hot and heavy, all hands with racing hearts and ragged breathes.

As I'm thinking these thoughts, I start to feel goose bumps come up on my arms. I ignore the sensation, thinking about being held in someone's arms and wish that I had someone that I wanted to hold…someone besides Peter. That's when things get interesting.

Trevor, a dark-haired, tall, thin student calls us to attention. I sit on the last row of bleachers so I don't have to climb in my skirt. He claps his oversized hands three times and everyone goes quiet. "As you know, we finally got the Swing Dance Club approved." Someone whoops, and Trevor continues. "We have a faculty sponsor, which was hard to find. No one dances like this anymore, so I can't tell you how lucky we are. So," Trevor presses his palms together. "Is there anyone here that has a basic understanding of Swing? Maybe you know the steps well enough, but nothing fancy."

I lift my hand along with a few others, most of whom are girls. We put our hands down as Trevor looks around and nods at each of us. "Okay, great. I was hoping that would happen. It'll help us get started, which is always the hardest part of forming a club. Until we have the basics, we really can't get into advanced moves, and we sure can't do throws. I don't suppose anyone in here is up to that level?"

I lift my hand, shyly, and wave my fingertips at him. He looks surprised.

"Jersey girl can dance?"

"Well, not alone. It's not like I can do anything more than the basic steps without an experienced partner." I rub my hands nervously in my lap. Everyone is looking at me. I squirm in my seat a little bit until a voice makes my heart skip a beat.

"How experienced are you, Colleli?" Peter says, rounding the bleachers from the side.

My mouth falls open. I glance at him and then back at Trevor, who introduces him. "This is Dr. Granz, our sponsor. He's also very experienced. This is great! Maybe you guys could show us a thing or two?"

Until then, I'd been staring at Peter. It isn't until Trevor offers me up, that I come back to myself. I act shy, and shake my head, saying, "That's okay. I'm sure we should just start with the basics tonight anyway." My heart is thumping in my chest, flopping around like a fish out of water. I can't breathe. I can't dance with Peter. Every time he touches me, my brain melts. The night we were almost together will come rushing back. I can't do it.

Peter cuts his gaze from Trevor and takes in my reaction. "We should stick to the basics. Advanced moves are very challenging. A novice would have issues and we don't want to single anyone out. Now—"

"I'm not a novice." I interrupt, offended. Peter turns his face toward me and I realize that I've been played. Bastard.

He's smirking. "Would you like to prove it?"

"Damn right, I would." I get up and smooth my skirt, annoyed with him. If the arrogant prick thinks he can do this better than I can, he's got another thing coming. Peter turns on the music. It's something newer, but it's still big band music—it's still swing.

We walk up to each other and lock eyes. It's as if I'm daring him to touch me. Peter's hands slip into place and we start.

Our feet move in step with each other. I pull and move, trying to take the lead, testing him. Peter won't let me. He dances me across the gleaming wooden floor, snapping my wrist back every time I try to defy him and move in a way he doesn't want. Peter's grip on my hand tightens, before he launches me into a spin. I shoot out from his body and twirl on my foot, before he stops me. Our hands are connected. He waits a beat and then yanks me back to him, hard. I smirk and spin back.

Okay, so he doesn't suck. That's when he kicks things up a notch. Our bodies move closer together as the music slows for this middle section. He plays my body, moving his hands down my sides and dips me back slowly until my long hair dangles to the floor. The faster rhythm resumes and Peter surprises me. I'm smiling now. I can't help it. We rock-step and twirl our way around the room. The students watching cheer and whistle. This is what they came here to learn.

The next time Peter whirls me against his chest, he holds me tight. His muscular forearm is across my chest as he presses my back tightly to his body. I hear his voice in my ear, asking, "You up for throws?" I nod, without hesitating. He releases me, spinning me out.

"Do it," I say, breathless. The pounding inside my chest won't stop and I can't wipe the smile off my face. The song is almost over and I wonder what kind of move he's going to do. When he shifts his hands, I follow his lead and I know.

Peter swings me out and snaps me back. When I race toward his chest, his hands slide from my arms to my waist. I grab hold of his strong shoulders and feel the momentum. Peter guides me, leading the move. My legs kick straight back up behind me. I feel the air catch my skirt, forcing it up. Peter's hands hold me tight as I glide back down. Peter guides my body so that my legs wrap around his waist before he dips me back.

The music crescendos and ends with us in that pose—eye to eye and breathing hard. A thin sheen of sweat covers my body. I'm suddenly very aware of his hands and my thighs. It's the way we were the other day, right before he pushed me away. Peter seems to realize this, and sets me down. His hands slip off my body and he turns back toward the other students.

Breathing hard, he says, "Start with the basics. No throws. You guys haven't signed the waivers yet." I watch him walk across the gym and grab water from a cooler.

Turning away, I wonder how bad that just looked. Everyone had to be able to tell how much I want him. I couldn't hide it, not with his body pressed against mine like that. I sit down on the bleachers and Millie slips next to me, overly excited.

"That was so awesome! Dude, you were like all," she makes a movement with her arm, "and he was all...OH MY GOD! It was so cool! I would die if I could dance like that. Why didn't I know you could dance like that?" Her eyes are bugging out of her head.

"Uhm, you did." I say, looking at her. "You dragged me here because I love swing dancing, remember?"

"Ah, so you were an unwilling participant this evening?" Peter appears from over my shoulder. He holds out a bottle of water for me. I take it, crack open the cap and drink.

Millie answers for me. "I dragged her here. It's for her own good. She's going to turn into an old maid if she doesn't find some guy to drool over soon."

Peter says nothing. His eyes are on my face, but I don't look up. Millie talks too much.

Trevor has taken lead of the class and Millie bounces off to rock step with Brent. They step on each other, a lot. Every time it happens, Millie stops and laughs.

Peter sits next to me. "So, old maid, I wouldn't have pegged you for a swing dancer."

"Yeah, well…Don't judge a book by its cover and all that." I don't look at him. I drink my water and watch the newbies kick each other as they try to dance together. I lift my chin, tilting my head towards the couples dancing. "This club should have shin guards."

Peter laughs. "Yeah, right. We weren't even allotted a budget for water and I had to fight with them to get this lovely building." His eyes flick to my face. "As you can tell, when April comes around, we're all going to be sweating buckets."

A bead of sweat rolls down my neck and between my breasts. I'm dripping way more than I'd like already. April is going to suck. "Maybe we can borrow a class room? There aren't that many kids here."

"Trevor thinks that it'll grow pretty fast."

"Does he?" I ask, looking at the guy.

"Yeah, he said there was a lot of interest, but no one comes in the beginning. It's the kind of thing people don't want to start, but they're happy to come once there are enough people to dance with."

I can barely understand what he's saying. All rational thought has left my brain. Damn, he smells so good, even covered in sweat. As Peter speaks, I act as though he has no effect on me, but he does. Every word he says pulls me to him. And it's the whole package, not just his looks. Why does he have to dance too? And he's good. I loved every second of it. If we practiced, I bet we could do more complicated moves and I'd love every second of that too. How pathetic is this? I'm crushing on my teacher.

"Yeah, I suppose so." I nod before getting up, trying hard to make it look like I don't care what he does. "Well, off to mingle with the masses."

As I'm walking away, Peter calls my name. "Sidney." His smile fades, but there's still a sparkle in those beautiful blue eyes. I look at him, waiting for him to say something, but he just shakes his head and looks away, "Never mind."

I want to know what he was going to say, but I don't ask. *I don't care. I don't care. I don't care.* Maybe if I say it enough times, I won't care about Peter Granz.

CHAPTER 11

Millie is twirling down the hallway when we get back to the dorm. She spins in a circle with her arms out, laughing at the ceiling. Her hair flies out in a circle. She's smitten. "That was so much fun!" Millie whirls into a girl walking out of a dorm room, nearly knocking her over. Millie makes an *oof* sound and then steadies the two of them, apologizing. I try not to laugh. The girl storms away irritated. It's late.

"And you!" Millie says, catching up to me. I didn't stop during the ambush. "I had no idea you could dance like that! You've been holding out on me."

I glance at her. "No, I haven't."

"Don't give me that, Little Miss Goodie Two-Shoes. You're always all pure and wholesome, and then you go and dance like *that*."

I stop and turn to her. "What are you talking about? Dance like what?"

Millie shimmies her chest and says, "All sexy, rubbing up against the hot teacher." She laughs hysterically, not knowing that I nearly slept with him.

I roll my eyes and keep walking. We round the corner and I pull out the key to our door. "I was not." Twisting the key, we head in and I drop my stuff on my bed. I don't know why I'm protesting. Peter is hot and the dancing makes me smile if I think about it too long, which means I can't let myself think about it at all.

Frickin' Millie and her observations. I glance at her. She points at me with a flick of her wrist. "You straddled the guy. Your thighs were around his hips."

She walks over to her bed, not paying attention to me. "You can't tell me that wasn't hot, because it was totally hot. Besides, he seemed to like it." I chuck a pillow at her. It hits Millie in the side of the head. She turns toward me. "Well, he did!" She throws it back.

The pillow hits the wall and falls on my head, knocking down a picture frame on my nightstand. I reach out and grab it before the frame bounces off the bed, and hits the floor. Setting it on the ledge next to me, I say, "You're impossible. Next time, I just won't come."

"You know you want to. And, I think that I'll ask you guys to show us more of that throw—in slow motion." She winks at me with her mouth open. It's all innuendo.

Stupid Millie. I'm close to laughing because her mouth hasn't shut yet and she keeps winking at me, waiting for me to giggle. I fold my arms over my chest. "Go ahead. I won't be there anyway."

"Yeah, right. You know you won't let me down." Millie shifts in her bed and sits on her knees. She looks at me funny for a moment.

"What?"

Her pretty face is all scrunched up. Millie holds a pillow to her chest and gives me a serious look. "You never let me down.

I mean, you always try to do what I want." She picks at the corner of the pillow, not looking up at me.

Something doesn't feel right. It doesn't sound like praise, like *oh Sidney, you're the bestest friend I ever had!* It sounds as though she's worried or something. It makes me nervous. I have no idea where this conversation is going. "So?"

"So, I have a question for you." She takes a deep breath and jumps in. "Why do you go on dates with me if you have no intention of dating? I mean, we've been roommates since freshman year and you haven't hooked up with a guy once, but you always come out with us when I ask you." Her voice is too serious.

Worry pinches my throat, making it hard to swallow. My mouth goes dry. I wonder if she knows what happened. My ex wasn't stupid enough to post what he did to me on Facebook, but there were pictures. They were the type of pictures that look wrong.

I feel her gaze on my face. I don't look up.

Millie finally asks, "Sidney, do you have a crush on me?"

Shock shoots across my face. I glance up at her and blink. "What?"

There's a half smirk on Millie's lips. Her eyebrows are doing this weird thing where one is up and the other is down. She looks right at me and adds, "I mean, if you're into girls, that's okay. I mean, I'm not—not that I don't like you—well, not like that. I was just—"

My eyes are too big for my head. She's rambling. Oh my God, this is so not what I thought she was going to say. My jaw drops open. I listen to her eat her foot and finally blurt out, "I'm not a lesbian."

Millie counters, "But it'd be okay if you were."

"But I'm not!"

Mille presses her lips together and considers me for a moment. It's as if she can't figure me out. Damn, have I become so dysfunctional that she can't tell I'm into guys?

She finally asks, "Then, what's up with you? Did your parents send you down here with a chastity belt or something?" She leans back against the wall and pulls her knees to her chest. "You don't date, unless I drag you with me—and honestly, straddling teacher-guy was the most action you've gotten since we met."

My face flames red. "This conversation passed the acceptable limit before it started." I laugh nervously and stand. I walk over to my closet and fish through it, looking for PJs.

"I'm serious, Sidney. It's like you don't think you should be happy or something. There's always this massive weight on your shoulders. I used to think it was because you're from New Jersey and everyone there must be super pissed-off all the time, but that's not it. Is it? You lit up when you were dancing tonight. I saw another version of you that I haven't really seen before. It's as if there's another Sidney locked away somewhere."

I stare at her. This isn't something I talk about. It's not something I share. Not after what happened last time I told someone. Part of me wants to say it. I want to know if she thinks that it was my fault, but I couldn't bear that. Not again. Shaking my head, I look away. "I just like dancing. It makes me forget to scowl all the time."

"One day, you'll tell me. And when you do, I'll be a good friend. You've been a good friend to me. You deserve to have someone to tell your secrets to, no matter what they are." She smiles sadly at me.

I can't. I feel the words lodged in my throat. I feel the bear at my back, but it doesn't matter—I can't say it. I can't tell her what happened to me, what he did to me. There's a span of silence. Neither of us moves.

Finally, Millie's gaze drops to her bedspread. "I think he might be the one."

Shocked by the abrupt conversation change, I don't follow at first. "Who? Brent?"

She nods. "Yeah. We get along really well—better than anyone else. I really love him."

"Have you guys said that to each other, yet?"

Shaking her head, she says, "Not yet. I nearly said it tonight. I'm thinking about it. It's hard, you know. Being the first one to say *I love you* is rough. I mean, he might not say it back."

"He'll say it back." There's certainty in my voice. I smile at her and she looks less fragile.

"How do you know?"

"It's all over his face, Millie. He adores you, even if he can't say the L-bomb, yet."

She smiles. Hard. It lights up her face. Millie leans back into her pillows. I change and then grab my books and try to get some reading out of the way, but my mind is elsewhere. I wonder how long it will be until Millie figures out what happened to me. Maybe I should just tell her and get it over with. When I realize that I'm no longer reading, I shut the light off and climb into bed.

This time when I close my eyes, I'm granted a reprieve. Instead of reliving the same nightmare over again, I see Peter's easy smile. I fall asleep thinking about my body twirling and his strong hands guiding me.

CHAPTER 12

A few weeks roll by and the last of the winter weather is gone. Spring is here. Trees are budding and there are flowers everywhere. The campus is covered in bright, beautiful, colors. It seems to make everyone extra smitten. Couples walk around totally love-struck, not paying attention to anything but each other.

Working for Peter has gotten better, less uncomfortable. I hate to admit it, but I like him. He's a good teacher and laid-back most of the time. It works out well since I'm usually as tense as a totem pole. Being around him soothes me. I don't feel as on edge as I usually do. I wonder if he notices things like that. Sometimes I think Peter doesn't notice much, but I think that's what he wants me think.

It's nearly dinner time. I'm on my way to my night class, but stop to check my mail first. I wave at a few people as I walk into the campus center and find my mail box. I turn the little lockbox dial, pull open the door, and yank out the mail. I slap the door shut and walk over to the table to sort it and toss junk mail.

Dusty sees me. He walks over and stands at the table opposite me. "Hey, Sidney."

We haven't spoken since our ill-fated date, which has been hard to pull off since he's in one of my classes. "Hey."

"I need to apologize. I screwed up the night we met. I shouldn't have—"

I so don't want to talk about this. I wave my hands, motioning for him to stop. "No, it was my fault. I—"

"It was not your fault. Come on. Let me say this. I've been trying to say it to you for way too long." I look at him and nod even though I want to bolt. "I was an ass. I shouldn't have assumed anything, but I did. I'm sorry, Sidney."

I glance at the mail in my hands as he speaks. Dusty's words are familiar. I've heard them before from another set of lips, from someone equally sweet. Appearances can be deceiving. I look up at him and nod. "Okay. Do me a favor though and let's just start over?" I don't want to start over, but he's been following me around, trying to apologize for too long to blow him off.

Dusty smiles. "Sounds good." He looks at the mail in my hands and then back up at my face. "You headed to class?" I nod. "Me too. I'll walk over with you."

Great. "Uh, okay. Sure." As I wait for Dusty to check his mail, I look at the letters in my hands. I toss a bunch of junk mail and then freeze on the last envelope. I recognize the handwriting. I stare at it, unblinking. A wave of shock nearly knocks me over. *He found me.*

"Ready?" Dusty asks.

I stuff the letter into my book, and nod. As we walk to class, I don't say much. Dusty talks and I listen, or try to….but that letter. Oh my god. It's been over four years.

Why would he send a letter? Why now? I'm nervous, so tense that I don't realize that we've entered the classroom and that Peter is talking to me.

Peter's hand lands on my shoulder and I jump. My feet literally trip back and I gasp. Peter steps back and lifts his hands, showing me his palms. "Easy, Sidney. Are you all right?" He looks concerned.

The class is watching us. I feel eyes on me. Too many people are looking. I find my plastic smile and put it on. I nod and laugh about being spaced-out. Dusty laughs with me, but Peter doesn't buy it. He doesn't tell me, in fact, he says the opposite. Peter even smiles, but I can read him. He'll ask me about it later, after everyone leaves.

It feels like I'm wearing a turtleneck made of thorns. I can't swallow. I can't breathe. Every time I touch my textbook, I feel the letter through the pages, burning a hole in my hand. I shouldn't read it. I shouldn't.

But what if it's important? What if—?
Don't read it. It's not worth it.

The internal debate continues in my mind. I stare blankly. The lesson continues around me, but I don't notice. Students talk. Someone laughs. A girl's voice rings in my ears a few moments later, but I have no idea what she said or what Peter said. The letter consumes me.

My palm is pressed to the pages. My fingers twitch. Halfway through class, Peter calls on me. I don't hear him. My gaze is on the floor and totally vacant. I don't realize he's standing in front of me until I see his shoes. I look up. "Sorry. What was that?"

He smiles at me and points to my textbook, which is open to the wrong page. Peter gives me a look, but doesn't say anything. "We're talking about poems. Dusty said they're emotional crap used to lure in women, that no guy in his right mind would ever write a poem on his own without an incentive."

I blink. "An incentive?"

Dusty is sitting two rows behind me. "He's saying it nicely. What I said was that no guy would write a poem for no reason. The poet in this case obviously wanted to get laid."

"Very eloquent," Peter says, and shakes his head. Folding his arms across his chest,

Peter looks down at me. "And what do you say, Sidney?"

I make a face and look back at Dusty. "Not that." I turn back to Peter. "A poem is an expression of emotions. It's condensed language. At its core…" My vision goes black at the edges. I wrote poems. I vividly remember what happened the day I wrote the last poem. The choking sensation doesn't stop. I can still feel his hands on me. I swallow my gasp and ignore the cold sweat on my back. Clearing my throat, I add, "At the core of poetry is purity—pure emotion, pure desire, pure elation, pure—"

Dusty speaks out, "So a poem can't be filled with lies? What if the guy just wants to nail you? What if it's all pretty words? You really think that ancient guys didn't write this stuff to get a little action? Come on, Sidney, you're smarter than that."

Dusty's words echo in my mind, wakening memories long buried. I clutch the side of my face and sputter, "Oh, come on, yourself. Not every guy is a bastard, Dusty. Isn't it possible that some poems were written because they were cathartic and had nothing to do with panties?"

He says something back. A few guys chuckle. I close my eyes hard, but the classroom tilts to the side. It doesn't stop. Dusty's words ring in my ear, as a buzzing sound grows louder. What the hell is the matter with me? It's just a letter. Dusty's just a dick. I already know that. Nothing is going to hurt me, but I feel so threatened. I chase away the panic that's consuming me and finally hear Dusty again. "...they did it then and they do it now. Guys don't write poems for themselves. They do it to get laid. If they need an emotional outlet, they punch shit."

For some reason, this conversation dredges up everything. Before I know what's happening, I'm gasping, clutching my desk so hard that my fingers turn white. Peter is watching me. He doesn't move. He doesn't silence Dusty. I stare at Peter's shoe and try to take long steady breaths. I'm going to have an anxiety attack and freak out in class. My heart is pounding, beating way too fast. A bead of sweat drips next to my ear and rolls down my jaw.

Peter cuts off the conversation. "So all the men in this room feel that way?" I hear movement, but don't look up. "Very well. For the rest of this class period you are to go to the library and write a poem. It cannot be for a woman and it has to be an expression of emotion. It's due on my desk at the end of the period. Bring it back here. Got it?" There's a lot of groaning, and then the sound of chairs moving.

I try to push back and stand, but I barely move before Peter says, "Sidney, I need to speak with you. Stay put for a moment."

Peter follows the class out of the room, and answers a few questions, telling them to return at 9:20pm with the poem. He tells them if they put in the effort, they get credit. No, length doesn't matter. A few guys snigger about the size not mattering. Peter responds by telling them that they have to turn in two poems. I hear curses and then silence.

No one is in the room. At some point, I laid my head on the desk and closed my eyes.

"Sidney?" Peter's voice is gentle. When I open my eyes, he's kneeling in front of my desk. His eyes sweep over my face, worried. I feel like I've been hit by a truck. "Are you all right?"

I sit up and nod. "Sorry. I don't know what…"

Peter's gaze is filled with concern. He reads me perfectly. He knows that I'm lying. I see it in that sad crooked smile he gives me. "You don't have to tell me anything. I just wanted to make sure you were all right. You're still pale. Sit for a while." Peter stands and walks over to his bag, and pulls out a Hershey bar. He walks back to me and holds it out. "Here, eat this."

I take it and sit up straighter. I'm hoping I can blame this on low blood sugar. "You carry around chocolate in your briefcase?"

He smirks as I bite into it. "Maybe. Truth is, that was going to be my dinner."

"Oh." I go to hand it back to him. There's a big bite mark in it. I have a huge mouth. Peter's hands brush against mine. Gently, he pushes the candy back to me.

"You finish it." His hands are still on mine. Peter looks into my face, trying to catch my gaze. "What set you off? It was as if you were somewhere else for a minute."

I don't look at him. Shoving the candy bar in my mouth, I bite down. The chocolate tastes like sand. I can't think about it. I try to push away the past, but I'm caught in a bear hug. The beast has left the leash. I'm speaking. I don't know why, but I nod. "I was. I'm sorry. It reminded me of something."

Peter squeezes my hands. I glance up at him and our eyes lock. My stomach flutters. He holds my gaze and doesn't look away. Peter breathes, and his voice is so soft. "Can I help you?" My gaze shifts back and forth between his blue eyes. I press my lips together and fight off the emotions he's making me feel. I can't feel them. Not now. Not ever. I shake my head so softly that I hardly move.

A sad smile moves across Peter's lips. "I wish I could." I say nothing. I can't speak. I have no voice. I just stare at his dark blue eyes. It feels as though I let the lifeboat sail away. I'm drowning in a sea of pain. He reached out, but I can't take his hand. I can't tell him what happened, and he can't fix it. Even if Peter knows, no one can change the past.

A girl walks in behind him. I barely notice her. "Dr. Granz?"

Peter startles and turns around. The girl doesn't think his behavior is strange, but Peter is too nervous. I see it. I see the way his shoulders tense, the way he slips his hands into his pockets, and the way he steps between us. She's holding her text book, asking something about Iambic Pentameter and rhyme schemes. He tells her that neither is required for the assignment. The girl's head nearly blows up.

Peter answers her questions as I finish my candy bar. When I'm done, I go to stand up. Peter points at me and says, "I can't let you leave. Sit. Finish the assignment in here."

"I'm fine," I protest, but my voice is wrong. It doesn't come out when I try to speak at a normal volume.

The girl looks back at me. "You look feverish. Do you need an aspirin or something? I have one in my purse."

"No, thanks, I'm okay." Aspirin won't fix what's wrong with me.

The girl nods and walks to the door. Before she leaves, she looks back. "Better do what he says or you'll end up in the nurse's office overnight. I've done that before and it sucks. The cots are horrible."

I nod and watch her walk away. Glancing at Peter, I say, "I'm fine. Really."

"You're a horrible liar. Just sit and write your poem. I won't bother you."

I want to say that he always bothers me. I want to say that he's a huge distraction, but I don't. I roll my eyes and pull out a sheet of paper. I start writing without thinking. It isn't until I'm done that I realize what I've written.

I'm staring at the page when Peter looks up at me from his desk. "Done already?"

I laugh. "No. I'm going to rewrite it." I crumple up the page and toss it. The paper sails through the air and bounces off the side of the trash can by the door, and falls on the floor. I jump out of my seat at the same time as Peter. We both head toward the paper, but Peter gets it first.

He smoothes it out. "I'm sure it's fine. It doesn't have to be perfect. The purpose was to—"

My stomach is crawling up my throat, and ice is dripping down my spine. I'm stupid. I'm so stupid. I could act like it's nothing and maybe he won't even read it. But I know if I fight with him, if I try to take the paper back, he'll know how messed up I am—he'll know the things on the paper are more than just a creative exercise. Why did I write that?

Peter's smile fades as his eyes fall to the page in his hands. He stills. His eyes don't move. It doesn't look like he's reading, but I know he sees it. Peter lifts his gaze slowly. I'm holding one arm with my hand, digging my nails in so hard I'll draw blood. "Sidney—"

"I don't... " my mouth is open, but the rest of the words won't come. *Deny it. Say that it doesn't mean anything. Say it.* But I can't. I can't even look at him. I don't say anything. I'm trembling even though I try not to move. It's like a chill has swallowed me whole. I'm frozen. Every muscle in my body is locked. I can't speak, I can't move.

This shouldn't have happened. I can't handle it.

Peter is staring at me with his eyes so big and blue. If he didn't see straight through me before, he does now. Peter looks at the paper in his hands. His grip is loose, as if the poem might bite him. "I had no idea..."

"Stop." My voice shakes. I curse my body, curse the memories that never fade away. "Don't, okay? It's nothing." I don't look at his eyes. My gaze is locked on Peter's chest. If I look into his face, I'll crumble. "It doesn't mean anything. It's just a bunch of words on a piece of paper."

I try to sound as though it's nothing, as if I write intense poems all the time. I pretend that I didn't just bleed my heart out onto a sheet of loose leaf. What the fuck is wrong with me? I pretend. I throw on my fake smile and stare at his shoes. I try to lift my gaze, but it feels like there's an elephant sitting on my head.

"That's not what this is." Peter's eyes are locked on my face. I'm breathing too fast, but every time I try to slow it down, it just gets worse.

"How would you know what it is or what it isn't?" I look up at him. *Mistake*. His expression, those haunted blue eyes, the curve of his mouth, the way he looks at me—it's like he knows. My fingers twitch by my sides. "I'm not standing here. I'm not having this conversation with you. I don't have to listen to you pretend to care about me." I turn around to grab my books. I gather them into my arms and head toward the door.

Just as I'm about to pull it open, Peter says, "I'm not pretending."

His eyes are on my back. My spine is so stiff and so brittle. There's too much pressure on me. I'm cracking, splintering in a million different directions at once. There's not one weak spot anymore. Weakness consumes me whole. "Don't say things like that to me."

Peter steps closer. I hear his steps traveling toward me. Slowly, he takes another step. His voice catches in his throat when he speaks. "I didn't mean to hurt you that night. I wasn't myself—"

"Neither was I. It's fine."

"But it's not." Peter's directly behind me. I won't turn. It doesn't matter what he says. *I don't care. I don't care. I don't care.* "I didn't know, then. I didn't know how smart you are. I didn't know you hide behind that sharp tongue. I didn't know why you were down here, and I had no idea why you sat down at my table, but I was glad you did. I've thought about that night over and over again. I wonder what would have happened to us if the phone didn't ring. I wonder what it would feel like to hold you again. I think things that I shouldn't. I dream things that I shouldn't. I want things that I shouldn't and it's all because of one reason—I *do* care about you."

I gasp as if someone punched me in the stomach. I hold onto the door to keep from falling over. I look over my shoulder at him. Peter means what he says. I see it in his eyes. Chills race over my skin. I stand there too long, staring at him in shock.

Peter taps the wrinkled paper in his hand. "Please tell me that this didn't happen in the last few weeks. Tell me that this isn't because of something that I did."

I stare at his face. I stare and drink him in like I'm dying of thirst. Shock has rendered me silent. My hand drops from the door. My lungs heave in air as I turn to lean back against the door. I hit it too hard and my weight pushes the door open. I start to fall backward. Peter reaches for me. His hands slip around my waist and he pulls me toward him, pulling me upright. The door clicks shut. He doesn't let go. His eyes are locked with mine. His body is pressed tightly against mine. Our gazes meet.

"Don't tell me that you're all right. I know you aren't... There's something about you." Peter takes a deep breath and lowers his gaze. When he looks up again, he says, "And I can tell."

My lips twitch like they want to spill my guts, so I lock my jaw. I shake my head and try to pull out of his arms. Peter doesn't allow me to step back. "Part of the poem is about you. Part of it isn't." Part of it's about Peter, and part of it's about *them*.

I'm hyperaware of my body, of my breaths that seem too long, but not long enough. I can't breathe. I haven't spoken about that night since it happened.

Peter's eyes remain fixed on my face. "The part at the beginning of your poem—the starting over, the tender kisses, the girlish giggles—that part is about me?" I nod. I hate myself, but I nod. "The part after that with the starving kisses, clawing hands, the taking without giving…" he's breathing hard. Peter's lips mash together before he speaks again. "This is about rape. Sidney, if some guy did something to you—"

I lean into him. I press my face against his chest. Peter's heart is beating so fast. "They're old wounds," I tell him. "I wrote without thinking. It's what poured onto the paper." I take a deep breath and pull away. Peter releases me. "That part had nothing to do with you or your *coffee* from that night." The corner of my mouth tugs up into a lopsided smile. It's the saddest smile ever. Peter's expression says as much.

He searches my eyes for a long time. We're no longer touching. I wish we were. After a moment, Peter offers me the paper. "I didn't read the whole thing. I don't think I was meant to see it. I didn't mean to…" he searches for the right word.

I take the paper and cut him off. "It's fine. I'm fine now." He gives me a look that says he doesn't believe me. "Really, I'm okay. I'm over it. Almost. Well, most of the time. Today just threw me, that's all."

"Why? What happened?"

I shrug and remember the letter in my textbook. "Remember how I told you that my family was pissed when I left?" He nods. "Well, that's true, but it was more than that." I glance up at his face, debating whether or not to tell him. The way he looks at me makes the words dislodge from my throat. They've been stuck there for years.

Before I realize it, I'm telling him my story. "I left. As soon as I got my scholarship down here, I packed a bag and drove away. I never went back. I didn't tell my family anything. I don't use Facebook or Twitter. I picked the worst place I could imagine to make sure they didn't find me. I did everything short of change my name. I thought it worked. No one found me. No one has called or said anything to me in four years..."

I slip the envelope out of my book and hold it between my fingers. "Until today. My brother sent me a letter. I got it right before class." I'm saying too much. I shouldn't tell him this, but I can't stop.

Peter watches me as I speak. I haven't told anyone any of this. No one here knows I was raped. No one knows anything. Shame flushes my face red and I look away from him. I hand Peter the envelope and sit down on top of my desk. My legs dangle down in front of me.

Peter takes the envelope and flips it over in his hands, before looking up at me. "What are you going to do?"

I shrug. "I don't know. Throw it out. Change my name." I stare at my shoes.

"Will he hurt you?" Peter is looking at the envelope when I glance at him.

I shake my head. "It wasn't like that. Oh God, I don't…" I stutter and rub my face with the heel of my hand. When I look up at Peter, I want to tell him. He makes me feel irrationally safe, as if nothing will hurt me.

"I never told anyone, besides my family." I'm quiet for a moment, remembering too many things that I want to forget. "I knew him, the guy that…" *raped me.* I still can't say it.

I suck in air as though there isn't enough and look away from Peter. "We were dating. I wasn't ready to have sex. He was. He took what he wanted. He said he'd do it again—that no one would believe me.

"I found my mom after the first time it happened. I told her. She told my dad. They did nothing. They said it was a date, that maybe I misunderstood or mislead him. My brother found out—I was dating his best friend—and said his friend would never do anything like that. They blamed me. All of them. They said it was my fault." My gaze lifts and connects with Peter's. "That was my senior year of high school." I smile, but it's angry. "You don't even know the sickest part. My parents liked the guy that did this to me. After that, they tried to keep us together."

"So, it didn't stop?" Peter's arms fold over his chest. His muscles bulge under his shirtsleeves.

I shake my head. "No," my voice is a whisper. Memories slam into me. I see a flash of silver as though it's really there. The story is so much darker. My fingers touch my throat, feeling the necklace that hides the scar. I can't tell him that part. I refuse to relive it. I push the thoughts back. My voice is soft. I twist my hands in my lap. "I didn't know what to do. I couldn't get away from him. And I didn't tell anyone else. My parents didn't believe me, why would my friends?

"So I switched my college without telling anyone. I found this place and they gave me everything I needed. I ran away and haven't looked back."

Peter says nothing for a long time. "You've had a hard life and I made it harder." His blue gaze pierces mine. "I'm sorry."

I swat away his apology. "You don't have anything to apologize for."

Peter shakes his head as he wraps his arms around his middle. "I led you on the night I first met you. I was going through some things, but I shouldn't have. And I sure as hell shouldn't have asked you to leave."

"You didn't."

"It was the equivalent of kicking your ass out." Peter sighs and runs his hands through his hair. "Listen, it's not an excuse, but you should know that it wasn't you. About a year ago, something happened. I lost someone. I'm not over her." His voice catches. Peter doesn't look at me. "I tried to move on and I wasn't—I couldn't. That's what happened the night we met. I couldn't tell you, then. I'm not sure I can tell the whole story now—"

I slip off my desk and walk over to Peter. Placing my hand on his, I say, "Then don't." I hear the pain in his voice. "You have a friend here, you know. University guidelines be damned."

Peter smirks and looks down into my face. "You care about me?"

"Maybe. A little bit." I hold my fingers really close together and grin. He smiles. I love that smile. "Well, that's not entirely true. I might like you—"

Peter cuts me off. "You *like* me?" Now Peter's grinning so wide that his dimples show.

"Not like that."

"No, you said it. University be damned. You like me. You *like me*, like me." Peter waggles his eyebrows, smiling at full wattage.

"I did not!"

"I believe you did."

"You're such an ass."

"Call me whatever you want, beautiful, but I know you like me." Peter walks behind his desk, bouncing on the balls of his feet with his hands behind his back.

"You're so arrogant. What makes you think that I like you? Maybe I'm just being friendly."

"Mmm hmmm," he says shuffling through some papers after he sits down. When Peter looks up at me, he adds, "You were very friendly, although I would have called being topless and in my lap something else." My jaw drops open. Peter grins. "Oh good. I was afraid that kind of friendliness was your typical MO. By the look on your face, I'm thinking that's not the case." Peter glances up at me. I sense the hesitancy in his voice. He wonders if he should tease me about it, but I'm glad he is.

It finally throws the whole damn situation out in the open.

"I was trying something new that night. You seemed to enjoy it." Heat flushes my face and I can't hide my wicked grin.

He winks at me. "I did."

"Jerk."

"Sexy."

"Ass."

"Beautiful."

"Agh!" I say, and stomp my foot.

Peter laughs. "Temper tantrum? Really, Miss Colleli?" Peter cocks his head to the side and looks at me. He's jotting something on a piece of paper and stashing his lesson plans back in his satchel.

"You infuriate me."

"Flattery will get you nowhere." Peter picks up his things and adds, "Come on."

"Where?" I feel light and happy, like I might break my face if I keep smiling this much. Peter brings out the best in me. The teasing has been going on for a while, but there hasn't been any mention of our sort of naked night before today. I don't know how he did it, but Peter chased away my demons. I feel as though I can handle things again, and I'm genuinely curious about where he wants to go.

"You owe me dinner and a glass of wine. I'm driving." Peter walks toward the door and looks back at me. I want to go, but we shouldn't. I hesitate. Peter gives a wry smile. "What happened to damning the university? Are you really all bark and no bite?"

"I'll bite you," I mutter under my breath and grab my stuff.

Peter grins. "You should. I'm very sweet, or so I hear—like candy."

"You probably painted yourself in chocolate."

"That'd work, but no. I've got this naturally sweet thing going on." He grins at me.

"You've got this naturally annoying thing going on. Have you been holding back for the past few weeks or what?"

"You've barely said two words to me since I took over for Tadwick. I thought you'd castrate me with the letter opener."

I choke on my spit and hack up a lung, before saying, "You did not think that!"

Peter shrugs and holds out his hand to the door, indicating that we should go. "What about the class?"

"There are directions on the desk. I'll come back later and pick up the papers."

"What about the University? Seriously, Peter, I don't want you to lose your job."

"I won't. I can have dinner with my students. It's not forbidden." Peter's serious for a moment. "I'll tell you what happened the other night. I owe it to you."

He doesn't owe me anything, but I want to hear his story. I want to know what's wrong with him. I want to know what kind of guy doesn't have sex with a girl that's already in his lap. There's something about Peter, something dark that's always just beneath the surface. Maybe that's why we get along so well. Maybe his life has sucked like mine.

Nodding slowly, I follow him out of the room.

CHAPTER 13

We go back to the same the restaurant as the night we met. It's fairly empty tonight. Between it being a weekday and the time, hardly anyone is here. The waiter seats us at the back of the room, on the far side of fireplace. I can't see the rest of the room from my seat. It helps me relax a little bit. Millie would never let me hear the end of it if she knew where I was.

Peter settles into his chair and we both order drinks. Peter sips some of the amber liquid from his glass, then says, "About the night we met—"

I'm mid sip when he speaks. I shake my head and swallow my wine. "Peter, don't. Really. That's not why I came." I don't need to rehash that night.

"Then, why did you come?" Peter's serious, as if he doesn't know.

"Because I'm hungry…and maybe because I like you. I thought we already established this?" I smile at him, expecting Peter to go back to his light-hearted self.

Peter watches me as I raise the glass back to my lips. "You're amazing."

"I know, right?" I grin at him. "I can hold a wine glass. Wahoo!" I hold up the glass by the stem and twirl it between my thumb and finger. The liquid inside swirls, but doesn't spill.

Peter smiles at me. The corners of his eyes crinkle when he does it, amused. "That's not what I meant, but your glass holding technique is impeccable."

I laugh. I don't know what it is, but there's something about Peter, something that puts me at ease. It's like I've known him forever, as if I could say anything and he'd understand. It makes no sense.

Our salads come out. The waiter puts them in front of us and then leaves. The food looks delicious.

Lifting my fork, I say, "I didn't get to eat here last time. I sort of freaked out, and attacked the waiter."

Peter holds a piece of lettuce on his fork and pauses. "No way."

"Way. My date had happy hands. I was trying to tolerate it, but I freaked out. It resulted in me jumping out of the booth like the place was on fire. I collided with that guy over there." The same waiter is standing on the other side of the room at the bar. "His tray fell over in slow motion. I'm pretty sure he's spitting in my food as they make it."

Peter's smile fades. "Why were you trying to tolerate a guy touching you?"

I shrug and stab my salad. "Because I want to be normal. In case you haven't noticed, I'm kind of messed up."

Peter gives me a somber look. "Actually, I did notice that you're kind of abnormal. For one, you have abnormally large eyes. They sparkle way too much. And that mouth of yours—well, let's just say that it's obviously defective." Peter smirks and picks up his fork.

"Shut up." I smile at him and shake my head.

Peter grins at me and waves his fork around as he speaks. "Being normal is overrated. Normal gets you what—the dolt husband with the 2.5 kids and the house with the dog? You seriously want that? I mean, one of those kids is going to be really funny looking, by the way, all cut in half like that. Who wants half a kid?"

I smile, but it fades quickly. I'm talking to Peter as if I know him, as if I've always known him. I don't worry about what he'll think. He won my respect and most of my trust in the classroom earlier. He didn't judge me. He didn't blame me. I haven't had a friend like that before, well, not a guy. Most of the time, I keep my mouth shut around guys. I don't want them to know me or what happened. I don't want to deal with it. Somehow Peter has helped me deal with it, and the emotions that were crippling me earlier have vanished. I don't know how he does it.

"I don't really know what I want anymore. I used to. But that wasn't what I meant by normal. Ever since it happened," I swallow hard and pause way too long. "Let's just say I have issues. I can't get close to anyone. I kind of thought that if I forced it, that things would get better." I don't look at him. I tried to force myself to have sex with him the night we met. He's hot and nice to touch, but my heart wasn't in it.

Peter's face pinches together. He doesn't understand. "You thought if you slept with someone that you didn't really like that you'd get over what happened to you?"

I flick my eyes up. "Well, when you say it, it sounds stupid."

Peter's staring at me with his mouth hanging open. "It is stupid."

"Wow, that was blunt." I poke my salad and shove it into my mouth.

"Sometimes blunt is better. So tell me, after you let this guy defile you, what happens next? You let him do it again?"

I stare at him. Good question, although it makes me wiggle in my seat. I stare at my salad for too long, but I feel Peter's eyes on me. His gaze is so intense. I shake it off. Peter starts eating again.

"I don't know," I say. "I thought it would help erase things. You know, push the memories that suck further back in my mind. There hasn't been anyone since him. I thought it would help."

Peter stops eating. His eyes are too wide. He looks at me strangely. His voice is low. "Is that what you were doing with me?" I don't answer. Peter smiles at me and shakes his head. He pushes the salad away and leans back in his chair. "Okay, I'm going to level with you." He presses his lips together into a thin line and then lets out a huff of air. His hands are on the table. His index finger is tapping the table top, nervously. "I was doing the same thing."

I tilt my head and say, "Yeah, right."

He smiles crookedly at me. "I'm not what they'd call balanced."

"Who's they?"

"I don't know," he shrugs. "Everyone. My mom, dad, sister, cousins, and other people who know me. I accepted this job and took off. They think I'm going to fall apart, especially after what happened." He lifts the amber liquid to his lips and drinks the rest in a single swig.

Peter sets the glass down. His eyes don't focus on me or anything else. It's like he's lost in a memory. "We—me and Gina—were in New York, seeing the stuff for Christmas. We went to Radio City and then to dinner. Afterward, it was late. She was ready to leave, but I wanted to go to Rockefeller Center. I wanted to get down on one knee under the tree and ask her to marry me."

He smiles. It nearly breaks my heart. I know that smile. It's a memory that's tainted, something that should have been happy but didn't turn out that way. I feel the weight of his story, the way he can barely say the words. He coughs and his eyes flick to mine. "I talked her into going. I was so excited. I couldn't wait to ask her. I didn't want to come back the next day. I wanted to do it at night, when the tree was lit. Gina loved Christmastime. I knew she'd love it.

"So, we get there and the place is pretty empty. It's late. While Gina was looking at the tree, I pulled out the ring. There were some people on the other side of the tree, but they couldn't see us. I kneeled and held up the ring." He breathes hard. The lines in his forehead crease. I can see the pain of this memory playing out across his face as if it's happening now. I want him to stop. Saying the words sounds like it's breaking him. I want to reach out and take his hand, but I'm frozen.

Peter looks up at me. His smile twists. "You're better at this than me. I've had a year to deal with this, but I still can't even say it."

"Peter..." I say his name and touch his hand. I catch his eye. "This really hot guy just told me a great piece of advice—it's stupid to rush things when you aren't ready."

He laughs once, hard. It makes his chest shake. Peter looks down at my hand. "That guy's usually an ass, or so I hear." He glances up at me from under dark lashes.

The corners of my mouth turn up slowly. "You heard right. He is an ass, a totally sweet, thoughtful ass. The best kind of ass really." I'm laughing lightly as I say it.

"Ah, your attempt at flattery is wasted."

I take my wine glass in my hand. "It's not flattery if it's true. You're a good man. Healing takes time. It's not the same for everyone. It doesn't happen at the same rate."

"Tell that to my family."

"Screw your family. They don't understand this—whatever happened to you guys. You do. You understand what happened and what it did to you. Talk about it when you're ready. Move on when you're ready." I finish my wine and put my glass down.

"It's easier to give advice than it is to take it, huh?" Peter watches me for a moment. His eyes sweep over my face, and rest on our hands. Mine palm is still on his. "So?"

I look where he's gazing and flinch. "Sorry." I try to pull my hand away, but Peter takes it and holds on.

"I'm not." Peter holds my hand to his lips and brushes a light kiss across my skin. It makes me shiver. He looks up and smiles at me. "We're trapped in the middle, you know. We're not in the friend zone, but we can't move forward."

I slip my hand away and nod. "I know," I say softly. "It's a good spot to be. A better spot than I've been in for a long time." I'm not out trying to bed some guy that I don't know. I'm not out with someone, doing something I don't want to do. For the moment, I feel perfect, unmarred. I feel like I might survive this with my mind intact. Hope floods my chest, and all my smiles are real. For the first time, in a long time, I think I'll be okay.

CHAPTER 14

At lunch a few days later, I grab a salad, some baked chicken, and sit down next to Tia. Millie hasn't come in yet. "Hey. How are your abs of steel?"

She gives me a look. "Soggy. I tried to do that video again last night. I'm not as sore today, but it still sucks." She plays with her fruit plate, poking the cottage cheese. "Screw this. I'm starving and that chicken looks good. I'll be right back." Tia's face scrunches as she stands. Her hand flies to her stomach before she stomps away to get a plate of chicken.

For a second, I'm alone. I hear his voice before I see his face. "Hey, sweetheart," Dusty says, and slides in next to me. "I heard something, and thought you'd want to know." I glance at him, wondering what kind of crazy sauce he ate to sit down next to me in here. He leans in and lowers his voice. "There are some awfully dirty rumors floating around about you." He looks delighted. His eyes sweep over me, lingering on my chest way too long.

What the hell? He irritates me, like seriously annoys me. I don't hate him, but I don't like him either. Glancing at him, I snap, "Who taught you manners? Give me your phone." I set down my fork and hold out my palm. I thrust it at him when he smiles at me. "Come on. Give it to me."

Dusty grins and pulls out his phone. "That's pretty much the rumor. The way you turned green the other night has everyone thinking you're knocked up and that the pretty professor did it."

What a jackass. I flip through his contacts looking for one in particular. "You seriously know how to flatter a girl. You called me fat and slutty in the same sentence." I press my thumb to one of his contacts and his phone dials.

Dusty finally notices that I'm not playing Angry Birds. "Hey, what are you doing?"

I hold up my index finger and shush him. Someone answers after a few rings. "Hi, this is Sidney Colleli. I'm sitting here with your son and I thought you'd be horrified at his manners. He really needs a once over before I smack my tray over his head." I called his Mom's cell phone.

She seems nice, but Dusty is hyperventilating, watching me as his thin body folds in half. He hisses, "You called my mom!"

Ignoring him, I nod and listen to his mother talk. "Yeah. Uh huh. He's right here." I look over at Dusty, widen my eyes, and smile.

"Hang up!" Dusty paws at me, trying to take the phone away.

I slap his hands and twist out of reach. "You heard that? I know. And he said that nicely compared to what he just told me."

"Sidney!" Dusty yells, trying to take the phone, but I don't let him get it.

"Yes," I continue my conversation with his mom, "I got sick in class last week. He implied it was morning sickness and blamed the professor. Uh huh. Please, that'd be great. Oh, I will." I laugh. "It was nice talking to you, too." I hand the phone to Dusty.

He looks at the iPhone like it's poison. "You suck."

"Yeah, well, tell it to your mom." I smirk and go back to my lunch. Dusty storms off, trying to tell his mom that it was a joke.

Tia sits down next to me with a plate of chicken and tacos. "What'd I miss?"

"Nothing worth repeating."

Tia stares after Dusty. "That kid is an ass. I don't know why Millie set you up with him."

I shrug and chomp on my chicken. "Millie's Millie."

"Who's talking about me!" Millie sits down next to us with a huge smile on her face. That smile scares the crap out of me. "Guess what night it is!"

"Oh, damn it. Millie, I'm not coming. I came the last four times."

She jumps up and down in her seat as if she's too excited to sit still. "But you have to! Swing Dance club wouldn't be the same without you."

"It wouldn't be a club without you," Tia nudges me with her shoulder and laughs while chewing on a chicken leg. Despite the predictions, the club is still pathetically small.

Millie glares at her. "You could come too, you know. It's hard to get a club started."

Smiling, I needle Tia. "You should. You and Jack would make such a cute couple."

Tia tenses. "Jack Ewing? He's there?"

Millie smiles at me and nods. Her blonde curls sway back and forth. "Yup, and he needs a partner."

"I don't know how to dance," Tia says, with a mouth full of food. "I'll look retarded."

Millie grins and then throws her arms around me, hugging me way too hard. "Sidney can teach us!" We nearly fall off the bench. I shake her off, and she laughs like a maniac.

Crap. I walked straight into that one. I sigh dramatically and narrow my eyes in her direction. "You suck."

"You know you love me." Millie squeals, smiling so wide that I can see all of her teeth. "So, you'll teach us a little before class tonight?"

Millie has her hands pressed together under her chin. Tia is watching me with that hopeful look in her eye. She's had a thing for Jack Ewing since last year. My resolve falters. "Sure. Why not?"

CHAPTER 15

That letter is still in my English textbook. I haven't looked at the book since class, and now I'm acting like it's been possessed by a poltergeist. I hid the textbook in my closet under all my clothes, trying to forget about it. I don't want the letter to touch anything else, but I can't bring myself to throw it away. My brother is a total ass, but he found me. It means something's wrong. I don't want anything bad to happen to them. It still stings that they didn't take my side, that they didn't defend me, but I don't wish them harm.

But the thing is, if I open that letter and find out what's going on then I'll be starting over again. I don't think I can manage the pain that goes with it. I don't want to rehash things. I don't want to tell them why I ran. I just want that part of my life to be over, but it's not. It seems as though it'll never end because it keeps popping up unbidden and unwelcome. Plus, my asshole ex-boyfriend was my brother's best friend. I don't know if he still is, but I don't want to reestablish any connection with him at all. All of them are dead to me. That entire life was burned to ash when I walked away.

My phone chirps, pulling me away from my thoughts. I look down at the screen. It's Peter.

Meet me at the gym at 6:15. I found a new move we can try.

I write back, *We r talking about dancing, right?*

Lol. There is absolutely no coffee *involved.*

That makes me laugh. I punch in, *Fine. I'll be there. C u later.*

So much for some down time. It's already getting late. I told Millie that I'd show her and Tia some basics before club. They're waiting for me downstairs. I'm wearing yoga pants and my hair is pulled into a messy ponytail. I'm not wearing make-up. In other words, I look as if I just rolled out of bed. I pad downstairs in my socks, with my dress shoes in hand.

Millie got the dorm director to give us the big living room so we won't kick each other quite so much. Based on last week's dancing, most of the club still needs shin guards.

I walk into the living room, not really paying attention. When I glance up, I stop in my tracks, and my eyes go wide. There are more than two girls standing waiting. There are more than twenty. "Millie!" I whip my head from side to side, looking for her.

Millie appears in front of me. She's grinning like she won the Miss America pageant. "It's awesome, right?"

"You said it was just me, you, and Tia," I hiss at her.

She realizes I'm upset. "What? Bigger isn't better? I thought more girls meant the club would attract more guys. And that's not a bad thing, right? Maybe we can find some closet swing dancers so you don't have to dance with Dr. Granz all the time." She winks at me. I stare at her with my mouth hanging open. I wonder what she meant by that, but I don't ask.

"You still suck." Millie smiles. Somehow telling Millie that she sucks has become tantamount to telling her that I'll do something.

She hugs me. I stiffen in her arms. "Sorry! I forgot about the no hugging thing." She holds up her hand and fist bumps me. I roll my eyes as she skips across to the front of the room and introduces me.

When I met Millie, she was a hugger. She hugged over everything. I didn't. We came to an agreement that hugs are reserved for prolonged partings and death. That's it. At least, I thought that was our agreement. It seems like she's figured out how to steal hugs more frequently. Millie's turned into a hit and run hugger. I don't know why she doesn't just give up on me.

Millie has gotten everyone's attention and is explaining the Swing Dance club, and how hard it is to get something new going. She tells them the basics and about the meeting later tonight, and then introduces me. "Sidney is so awesome at this. You'll have to come to club later and see her dance. I swear to God, you'll think she's amazing. So come on out! And I'll make sure we get enough guys there to make it worth dressing up."

"We dress up?" someone asks. It's Jen. She's an Asian girl with tan skin and silky black hair.

Millie explains swing clothes, and tells them that they probably already have a lot of that stuff in their closet, while I put my shoes on. I look so stupid. I'm wearing T-straps with yoga pants. I look really weird. At least there aren't any guys here. It's the only benefit of an all-girls dorm.

After Millie's done, she says, "All yours."

Nerves tickle up and down my arms. Hysterical laughter wants to burst from my mouth. I hate public speaking. Millie really sucks. My gaze shifts her way. Apparently Millie can read my mind, because she sticks out her tongue and then grins like a sadistic monkey.

"Okay, if you've been brought here against your will, blink twice." I'm joking, but a few girls blink. "Damn, I was kidding." A few people laugh and I realize that they're nervous, too. "I know how you feel, because I was under the impression that there'd be less people here, but let's make the best of it."

Millie cuts in, "Yeah, I kinda said we'd only have a few people, but when they found out it would just be a few girls, I ended up with more people than I thought. But I have to tell you—swing dancing is really fun. It's a great way to exercise - thrilling and sexy all rolled into one. Dancing is a way to get to know a guy, and I mean really get to know a guy. Everything from the way he leads you around the floor to the way he spins you, says something about him. I learned a lot about Brent after we finally stopped kicking each other." She laughs. A few girls smile at her.

"What about throws?" someone asks. "I've seen stuff where the girl gets tossed into the air."

I answer, "The throws are like riding a roller coaster without a seatbelt. Once you get the basics down, the club will move into more advanced stuff. Pe… Dr. Granz and I usually show off some advanced moves at the beginning of club. It helps you see what you're aiming to do. If that kind of thing appeals to you, we can work up to it."

After that, we get into the basics. I have the girls line up and start showing them how to count off the steps. That's all we do. For about half an hour we count and rock-step our way around the room. Toward the end of the class—or whatever it is I'm doing—girls pair off. They're pretty much kicking each other. They look up at me like I taught them wrong.

"This isn't working!" Tia says as she kicks Jen in the shin.

"Suck!" Jen curses and tries again.

Waving my hands at the front, I say loudly, "You've been taught the girl part. The assumption is that you'll be dancing with a guy. The guy's part isn't the same as ours. That's why you're kicking the crap out of each other. Listen!" I clap my hands and they all stop. "Later at club, if you want to dance with your friend, one of you needs to reverse your moves. And, the guy always leads."

"That's so sexist!" Someone calls out from the back of the room.

I smirk. "Yes, it is. And you need to make sure you dance with a guy later. The concept is one thing. Doing it in action is another." I'm a control freak, but dancing is different. It's a place to let someone else lead for a while. I wave and tell them that I'll see them later.

CHAPTER 16

I have just enough time to go upstairs and change before I see Peter. I run up the staircase and grab my stuff. After showering quickly, I twist my hair up into a high, sleek ponytail. Then I grab a sundress I found in a thrift shop. It's dark blue with buttons down the front. The V-neckline makes me look stacked. I'm not sure what I think about that part, but it fit so well and the skirt was perfect for this. I wonder if I should change—my cleavage is a bit much—but I'm running late. Besides, it's nothing worse than what the other girls wear. I just don't usually wear stuff this revealing.

I pull on a pair of bike shorts under my dress, and then put the T-straps back on. After swiping some mascara on my eyelashes, I look in the mirror. My cheeks are rosy. I don't have that listlessness about me anymore. I'm smiling. I don't even think about it, but I'm grinning, and I know it's because of Peter. Part of me is glad that things never progressed the night we met. He's turned into a great friend. I'm not sure if that would have happened if I slept with him. Well, okay, let's be honest. We wouldn't have been friends at all. Peter would have been an awkward acquaintance that I avoided like the plague.

As I leave my room, I bump into Tia. She's wearing a robe and her hair is wrapped in a towel. She's walking back to her room from the showers. "Hey, you heading over there already?"

I nod. "Yeah, Dr. Granz wanted to go over a move with me before you guys show up."

Tia's eyes dart to the side. She glances up and down the hallway and then leans in. "Is there anything going on with you two?"

I jerk away like she hit me with an iron. "What?"

"I'm sorry, Sidney, but I had to ask. People have been saying how hot Dr. Granz is and how much time you guys spend together. Someone said they saw you guys at the library, and then eating at the swank place across town." She shrugs her shoulders. "I told them they were crazy, that you wouldn't do something like that."

"But you asked me anyway."

She nods. "You're going to meet him early, to practice a dance that you said is sexual."

I sigh way too loud. "That's not what I meant. I was talking about you guys."

"So it's sexual for us and not you?"

"It's not like that." I don't have time for this and I can't understand why people keep saying it. "You can dance with your brother, right? There's a difference."

"He's not your brother, Sid."

"Whatever. I'm not sleeping with him, if that's what you're asking." I'm so irritated. I want to bite her head off. It's so hard not to. I keep locking my jaw as the conversation goes on and the weird thing is that I don't know why I'm so upset? So what if people think I have a crush on Peter?

But that isn't it. The crush isn't bothering me. It's innuendo, the broken propriety, and it'll get Peter in trouble. I don't want anyone questioning his morality. They can question mine. I'd wave my hand in the air and say that I'm a moral deviant to keep the attention off of Peter. Maybe I should do that.

My eyes flick up to Tia's face. I lean in, feeling the lie on my lips. Tia mirrors me and gets closer. "I have a crush on him, okay. But he doesn't encourage it. That's why we're together a lot. I'm stalking him."

She clasps her hands together under her chin and squeals. It sounds like someone stepped on a pig. The noise keeps going, getting higher and higher. I try to smile and bounce up and down the same way she is. "I promise I won't tell a soul. But this is so exciting. He's so much older! Oh, and since it's totally forbidden, it's insanely hot. I can't wait to see what this guy looks like."

I shush her. "Keep it down. I didn't even tell Millie. Don't say anything, okay. If things look weird, it's my fault. Listen, I have to run. I'll see you later." I glance at my watch and then dart down the hallway before she can say anything else.

―――

"Come on, Peter. Put the moves on me," I say as I walk across the old gym. I realize I'm flirting and feel a bit silly for a second. I'm not sure where it came from. When I saw him, I just wanted to tease him and have that banter I've grown accustomed to when Peter is around.

Peter is sitting in the bleachers, watching something on his phone. He looks up when I speak. "Colleli. You're late."

"I had to take care of something. I'm here now. What's this new dance you wanted to show me?" I sit next to him and look down at his phone. It's a couple dancing, doing the usual steps, twists, spins, and throws. It's a pretty good routine, actually.

"It's the throw at the end. I can't figure it out and I haven't seen it before. Watch." Peter's eyes slip over and rest on the side of my face for a moment before returning to the screen. My lips part as the couple gets to the end of the song. They're really good. I gasp when they perform a death spiral. The woman's head comes so close to the floor.

I start to ask if that's what he wanted to show me, but Peter says, "That's not it. Keep watching."

I watch. As the music crescendos, the dancers pull out all the stops. The last move is hypnotic. The woman is in the guy's arms and then he flings her out. It resembles a variation of the Hustle, but then they do something and she's suddenly airborne. The guy catches her as she twists in the air. They swoop down together and he holds her in a bow. Both dancers smile and the video stops.

"Holy shit." I blink like I didn't just see that.

"I know, right?" Peter says, looking baffled.

"What the hell was that? I mean, I've seen a lot of crazy dances, but that looked awesome. I'm not even sure what they did."

"Neither am I. That's why I wanted to show you. I've seen plenty of moves, too. This one is a variation of other stuff, kind of mashed together. That dip at the end looked like a modified death spiral."

I glance at him. "You realize this could be fake, right? I mean, how did she get that kind of height? He didn't seem to throw her, and she didn't jump."

He shakes his head. "It's not. This is a dance studio in New York. It's the video to used attract new students, so it shouldn't be fake."

"Play the end again." Peter rewinds the dance and plays it again. We both stare at it, trying to figure out what they did. Part of the problem is that the camera is at a bad angle. I can't see their hands right before the lift. I shake my head and point at the screen, saying as much to Peter.

"I know," he admits. "I was hoping we could figure it out." I give him a look that says, *hell no*. "What? No spirals?"

"I'm not doing anything with you where my head gets that close to the floor, so no."

"Why not? I thought if you were okay with throws, you'd be okay with this."

I shake my head and glance at the yellow wooden floor and think about getting my face ripped off if he drops me mid-spin. "No. No way."

"No way?" he's smiling. "Well, now we have to do it." Peter takes my hands and pulls me up off the bleachers.

I laugh and tug away from him. "You don't even know how to do it. You can't be serious."

"I'm always serious."

"More like you're never serious."

He laughs. "Yeah, that too." Peter folds his arms over his chest. He's wearing his white dress shirt, but removed the tie. Dark slacks cling to his narrow hips and those saddle shoes are on his feet. Dark hair hangs in his eyes. "No dips? No head dives?"

"Nope. Sorry."

"What if I gave you a helmet?" Peter's eyes sparkle a little too much. He's teasing me.

"Then I would definitely say no. The helmet means you expect my head to collide with the floor. Besides, it'll ruin my awesome outfit." I hold onto the hem of my dress and pull it out as if I'm going to curtsey.

"Ah," he says, walking toward me. Peter slips his hands around my waist and music clicks on. He starts dancing, pulling me along with him. "Then, there is a possibility."

"What part of no is confusing you? I thought you were an English teacher. You seriously have issues with this?" I'm smiling. I love teasing him. Peter's face lights up and he teases right back.

"First you said no, then you said defiantly no. So, I'm thinking there's wiggle room." He grins and pulls my wrist. We both spin, and then I follow his lead and shoot out from him. Peter tugs me back and I twirl into his chest and the dance resumes.

My breathing is harder. The dance is getting faster. "We're not wiggling anything."

"Are you sure? You'd look cute in a helmet. I have a pink one with a red bow on top." I stop dancing and try to stand there and stare at him, but Peter doesn't let me. "No stopping, Colleli." He snaps my wrist and pulls me to his chest. Damn, he smells good.

We swirl around the gym, talking, teasing. The subject rolls over a million different topics. Then, he asks, "Do you trust me?"

The smile slips off my face. My face is covered in a sweaty sheen and my dress is stuck to my body. I look into his eyes. They're locked on mine, waiting for an answer to a question that I thought he'd never ask. "I... don't know."

Peter nods and looks down at his feet. When he looks up again, I feel horrible. It's as though that was the worst thing I could have possibly said to him. "That's something I hope for." He rubs the toe of his shoe against the gym floor. His shirt is wrinkled, stuck to his chest.

"Why?" I breathe. It seems so pointless. Why would it even matter?

He smiles sadly. "I don't know. I shouldn't have asked you something like that."

"You can ask me anything." I look down at my hands. They're together and I'm twisting my index finger. "I guess, I do trust you to some degree, probably more than I trust anyone else, but I don't think that's what you're asking."

"What did you think I was asking?" He's so close. Peter stepped into the space between us. He's looking down into my face, watching me so closely. It makes me shiver.

"I thought you meant, do I implicitly trust you with my life. With a throw like that. With anything and everything." I shake my head. "I'll never trust anyone that way again."

He nods slowly. "You're an enigma."

The corner of my mouth lifts. "Maybe."

"You trust, but you don't. You let me in, but you keep me out." The way he's looking at me makes me nervous. Peter's gaze is so intense, so raw and vulnerable. Maybe I should have lied? No, he can see through me. He doesn't need dancing for that. Peter holds up his hands. I take them and he leads me across the room in a slower waltz so I can catch my breath.

"Can I ask you something?" I ask as Peter leads us across the room. He nods. "Where'd you learn to dance?"

A shadow creeps over his face and his smile disappears. "Gina. My girlfriend. I keep calling her my fiancé, but she wasn't." He swallows hard and lets out a rush of air. We turn around the floor as he speaks. "She liked to dance. I sucked at it. She taught me." He smiles sadly.

"She taught you well."

He nods and a fake smile lines his lips. I can tell that he's chasing away old memories with a broom. Peter's gone silent. We dance. He spins me slowly. My dress flares out around my knees. He watches the fabric flutter before pulling me back into position. "What about you? Who taught you to dance?"

"I'm self-taught for the most part. I don't really know what anything is called.

We talked my gym teacher into doing a unit on dance in high school. Weird but true. Way better than volleyball again. I can only get hit in the face so many times a day."

He laughs. "Volleyball's not your thing?"

"Coordination's not my thing."

"But, you're dancing."

I smile up at him. "And you're leading. It's different. For one, there are no balls." My face flames red when I realize what I just said.

Peter chuckles and shakes his head. "Well, I might disagree, but since we're not playing with them, I'll just pretend you didn't say it."

I try not to laugh, but I can't help it. I try to pull my hands away and slap him, but Peter grips me tighter. The playful smile slips off my face when he holds me that way. We stop moving and stare at each other. My lips are parted. There was something I was going to say.

Peter looks down at me, his face so close to mine. His breath tickles my lips as he breathes. I want to lean into him. I want his arms around me. I don't know what he's thinking. When time stops like this, Peter looks lost. His entire body tenses and relaxes at the same time. I wish he'd do something, say something.

All the air is being forced out of my lungs. "What are you thinking?"

"Nothing," he breathes, still watching me. His eyes flick back and forth between mine. His gaze doesn't dip to my lips.

A slow smile spreads across my face. "Liar." I lean in closer and press my forehead against his. "Just tell me."

Peter's hands find my cheeks and then slip back into my hair. He holds me for a second and breathes, "I can't."

"Peter…" his gaze lifts. I feel like he punched me in the stomach. There's so much there, so much pain and affection and turmoil. It kills me. I can feel his agony when I look into his eyes. I take his hands and put one on my waist. "Dance with me. Stop thinking for a while." He nods, and says nothing.

Neither of us speaks again. Peter leads me around the floor, changing the dance as we go along. We lose track of time. It isn't until I hear Millie's loud whistle that we stop. Peter nods at me and heads to the cooler to grab a bottle of water.

Millie walks over to me with her eyes bugging out of her head. "What the hell was that?"

I walk into the hallway to find the girl's room. I need to splash water on my face. "What was what?"

Millie follows me. She grabs my arm before I can push through the bathroom door. I whirl around. "You like him."

"I do not. We were practicing something. You'll see it in a few minutes. Let me wash my face off. It's too damn hot in there." I try not to sound bitchy, but fail. I'm too defensive, too fast to get out of there.

Millie opens her mouth to counter my claim and follows me into the bathroom. She looks under the stalls, and when she knows we're alone, she says, "Do not do this."

"I'm not doing anything."

"Sidney, don't lie to me. Can you honestly tell me that there's nothing between you two?" Her hands are on her hips. She's looking at me in the mirror.

"There's nothing. I don't know what you think you see, but maybe you should have your eyes checked." I splash water on my face. I have on waterproof mascara, but it'll run if I rub my eyes. I grab a paper towel and pat my face dry.

"You wouldn't say it that way if I said you were sleeping with Dusty."

"Uh, you're right, because I'd choke on my vomit. What's with you?" I turn around and lean back on the sinks. "You're the one who wanted me to come and do this. Peter's my boss. I'm his TA. And yes, I call him Peter the same way I called Dr. Tadwick, Tony."

"You called Dr. Anthony Tadwick, Tadwick. You never called him Tony, not to me." She looks concerned and she shouldn't be. Millie sighs and rubs the side of her head. "Just don't do anything stupid."

"God, why do people keep saying that?"

"Sidney, that's usually a pretty good sign that a big truck load of stupid is about to mow you down. Listen to your friends. Don't screw your prof. Sleep with guys your own age." She sounds like she knows everything, which pisses me off.

"How many guys have I slept with in the entire time I've known you?"

"I don't know? You want an exact number?" She's leaning toward the mirror, fixing her eye make-up.

"Just guess. Best estimate, based on lingerie, dates, make-up, and whatever else you can think of. Tell me how many guys you think it's been."

She's quiet for a moment and then shakes her head. "I don't remember hearing you talk about anyone like that."

"Am I talking about anyone like that now?"

"No." She shakes her head. "But that doesn't mean—"

"It doesn't mean what? Millie, what do you want from me? You set me up with guys, I tag along with you, I do every little thing you ask me to, and then I find some guy that I actually get along with and what? You're telling me to stay away from him?"

"He's a professor, Sidney. You're going to get in trouble."

"For what? For being his friend? For not sleeping with him? For not fucking him the first day he was here? Exactly what did I do wrong, because I'm not seeing it?" I'm yelling. I don't mean to, but I am. "You know what. Forget it. I'm not talking about this with you."

"You almost slept with him?" I shake my head and put up my hands, as if it'll deaden my ears to her words. "Sidney, wait." She chases me out of the ladies room and down the hallway. "Where are you going?"

I'm leaving the gym. I feel bad about ditching Peter, but I can't do this. I feel like I'm going to fall apart. I need to calm down. I slam open the doors to outside and go sit in the parking lot. I'm leaning against a car, and tuck my head so no one can see my face. I breathe deeply, trying to calm down. I left my phone and everything inside.

What the hell is wrong with me? Why did I flip out on her? Millie didn't say anything bad, not really. It wasn't like Dusty telling me the rumors. Maybe that's what's bothering me. I made the rumors worse.

Damn it. I sit on the car for a while, wondering how stupid I am. Maybe I shouldn't be hanging around Peter at all. It makes me sick to think about not seeing him every day, but maybe Millie's right. Maybe I should be going after guys my own age.

Am I really hung up on Peter? Is that why I haven't had a date since January? It can't be Peter. That's not it. There are plenty of guys that are hot. I should find one and start over. But why?

To be normal. To start over.

My life has been stuck on pause for way too long. No boyfriend, no dating, no swooning over some guy, wondering when I'm going to see him again. Unless I count Peter.

Don't count Peter.

The night air is thick. My dress is clinging to me. I glance down and notice my cleavage is glistening. Damn it. I look all whorish. I fan myself, thinking I'm alone. It's much more humid than usual, as though it might rain. Just when I think I'm ready to go inside, I see someone walking toward me.

"Hey, if it's not the techie TA." Mark from Peter's morning English class drops a bunch of books on the hood and walks over to me. I avert my gaze. My face is on fire. I feel the blush down to my toes. Holy shit, did he see me fanning my boobs?

He scooches next to me. "Are you okay?" He tries to get a glimpse of my face, but I don't let him.

I nod. "Fine." My voice squeaks.

He laughs. "Ah, cuz it looks like you're not fine, all avoiding my gaze like that. And, not fine has some obligatory obligations that go with it." He's leaning on his hands, and not looking at me. The way he says it makes me smile, but I still feel stupid.

I glance up at him. "Obligatory obligations?"

Mark nods, "Yeah, like tissues, totally. And maybe a ride home, 'cuz it would be lowly of me to make you walk." He ducks his head to the side and tries to catch my eye. I glance at him and give a weak smile. "That's better. Wait 'til you see the tissues. Prepare to have your mind blown." He moves around to the driver's side and comes back with a box. I thought he was kidding, but when he holds them out, I can't help it.

My jaw drops and I grab for one. "Wow. These are really tissues?" I feel the soft tissue in my hand, but the thing is glowing. I dab my brow and my neck. My body is covered in little beads of sweat. It's so frickin' hot.

"Yup. I got 'em off the internet. The only horrible side effect is that your nose, or wherever, will glow green for a while when everyone shuts out the lights."

I stop and stare at him. "What?"

There must be knifes shooting out of my eyeballs, because he holds up his hands and says, "Just kidding, pretty lady. I just wanted to see you smile again." Mark bumps his shoulder into mine. I can't help it, I grin. "There it is. You made my night. Please sit on my car anytime you want. It's usually unlocked. Feel free to sit inside, if it's raining or what-have-you."

I nod. "Thanks, Mark."

"No problem, babe. You want a ride somewhere?" He's so sweet. The guy has been around me all semester, but this is the first time he's really talked to me. During class, I've caught him looking my way, but I thought I imagined it. He's too cute and way too popular to be talking to me. I can see why there's always a group of people around him.

I look back at the gym. This guy is my age and he's really sweet, but...

"No, thanks. I need to head back in. But thanks for this." I hold up the tissues. "By the way, if my boobs glow green tonight, I'm gonna hunt you down."

He laughs so hard he nearly falls off the car. "Totally didn't expect that from you. But, feel free. Green boobs or not, you can hunt me down anytime." He smirks at me before ducking into his car. I watch him pull away, then head inside.

CHAPTER 17

I'm sitting on the bleachers when Peter sees me. He walks over and sits next to me. "I thought you ditched me."

"I thought about it, but I didn't want to make you look bad in front of all these kids. Millie pissed me off. Well, it's not Millie. It's everyone. They're talking." I'm picking at my nails as I'm speaking. When did I start telling him every little thing? I look at Peter out of the corner of my eye. *He's your friend, stupid. Of course you tell him stuff.*

Peter looks puzzled. "They're talking about what?"

"About us. I've heard everything from you knocked me up, to you're doing me in your office, and that TA means something else entirely. Get it? T and A? Har har. It's hysterical." I make a face and watch a couple of kids trying to dance in front of us. Another couple bumps into them.

Peter gives me a strange look and then laughs. He runs his hands over his head, rumpling his hair. "Damn. I finally have a platonic relationship with a woman and look where it gets me."

"I know right? You scoundrel, you." I'm leaning on my hands, with my elbows on my knees. There are more people here tonight. The music is blasting and the air is warm. Someone propped open the back door. The night air drifts in slowly and smells sweet, like honeysuckle.

"So, what'd you tell them?"

"I told one person that I have a mad crush on you. I kind of freaked out on her a little bit when she told me what people were saying. I needed a diversion. And Millie, well, I just bit her head off. No explanation." I stare straight ahead.

Peter clears his throat. I look at him out of the corner of my eye. He's grinning. "You defended me? And what, my honor? I thought I was supposed to do that for you?"

I smirk and turn toward him. Peter's face is glistening from dancing. Damn, it's hot in here. The no air conditioning thing is rough. My eyes drift to his shoulders and down his chest. Peter's shirt is sticking to his chest and is very wrinkled. He looks good. There's more color in his cheeks, more life in his eyes than when he first got here.

I bump him with my shoulder. "You're a dork, you know that?"

"Is it because of the dancing?" Peter asks, seriously, trying to figure out why people would say that about us. He looks baffled. Peter pushes his hair out of his face. It's damp and curling at the ends.

"Are you kidding?" I ask and he shakes his head. I smirk at him. "It's because you're hot. There'll be rumors about anyone you talk to unless they see you dating someone, and even then… well, people are stupid. They talk even when there isn't anything to talk about."

"Did they say things like that about Tadwick?"

"Tadwick wasn't hot. You are."

"And whose opinion is that?" He's grinning at me. Peter bumps me with his knees.

"It's the word on the street. Personally, I think you're a little too muscly and tan. I prefer my men frail and pasty. Sorry, Charlie."

"Peter. My name is Peter. Damn, Sidney. You can't even remember my name." Peter's smile deepens and I can see a dimple on his cheek. They're so cute. He is pretty to look at. I glance at a flock of girls behind him on the bleachers. There's a pool of drool on the floor. They are all staring, their mouths gaping like Swedish Fish.

I get up and smack Peter in the arm with the back of my hand. "Come on, professor. I want to dance until I can't stand up." I bound across the room with Peter on my heels. I stop and turn suddenly. He nearly slams into me. Time freezes for a moment. The air feels hotter, the night feels electrified. Peter lifts his hand. I press my palm to his. The touch is charged. I feel it down to my toes. I grin broadly. I can't help it. And we dance.

Peter's hands are always in modest places, but the way his hands slide over my skin and glide over my dress, well, it feels like he owns me—like I'm his to control. It's weird. I've danced before, but this feeling never emerged. I danced to get away from my ex and my family. They weren't interested. It was a place to find my balance and learn to endure my life. But Peter changed that. I'm no longer enduring. I'm laughing, sweating, and spinning. I don't shirk away from his touch, either. That's new. When we first started dancing together, I enjoyed it—I can admit that— but his hands made me nervous. Now they make me comfortable. I feel stronger, better.

The music moves faster as the tempo changes. We're laughing and some of the students stop to watch us. Peter asks as we dance, "Ready?" He wants to do a throw.

I nod. I expect him to lead into the steps, but he doesn't. Instead we step into each other and Peter spins me back and pulls me to him. I grin. "What are you doing?"

"Nothing. Just wondering why you trust me with throws but not—"

"Death spins? I think it has something to do with the word *death*." I laugh. The music pulses through me. Peter winds me around him and under his arm, then he snaps me back to his chest.

"I think I could convince you." He smiles down at me and twirls me across the floor. We separate for a few steps before he reaches for me again. I'm back in his arms. There's a not much space between us. Peter holds me so close that we're nearly touching.

"I'm not wearing a helmet."

He laughs. "You're so stubborn."

"You're so not going to throw my face at the floor." I grin at him. Peter holds up his palm and pushes on my back. I follow, moving under his arm. The music is in the right spot to lead into the aerial.

"Are you holding out on me or are we doing this?"

Peter yanks me close and my hips slam against his. My heart is pounding way too fast. "Let's do it."

Peter leads me into the move, and I follow. A twist, a turn, and he pulls me hard. I roll over his back with my legs splayed. My skirt flares and I land on the floor. I duck, and Peter swings his leg over my head before he pulls me up into a twist. I slip up from between his legs, and he lifts me by the waist. I continue the move and kick. I feel the momentum as I swing upward. I'm smiling way too big. My stomach has that free-fall feeling as I come rushing back down.

Peter executes the move perfectly and my legs fly around his waist. His hands cradle my back as dips me backward. The music stops. We're both breathing hard. The silence becomes more noticeable. Peter holds me for a moment. The club starts clapping and Peter sets me down. He nods at me, as if it was a demonstration. Then, he goes into safety issues with those kinds of moves and invites the more advanced dancers to learn some of the steps we just did.

A girl walks up to Peter. He holds out his hand and dances with her. That's when I realize that sharing isn't my thing. Peter looks beautiful, all rumpled and smelling like heaven. Stuffing my nail-clawing instincts back into the crazy part of my brain, I grab a bottle of water from the cooler. I watch him show a few girls the moves in slow motion. There are some guys there, too. He shows them where to put their hands and how to lead the steps.

I guzzle my water and walk the perimeter of the room, trying to cool off. After a while, I head toward the open door. The night breeze feels good on my skin. I step outside. The sky is deep indigo, like a bottle of ink. There's a speckling of stars tonight. I lean against the cool brick wall, feeling the rough stones through the thin fabric of my dress.

A few moments later, Peter comes out. "Dinner?"

"Sure. I didn't get a chance to eat, yet."

"Good." He nods and heads back inside.

I'm standing there for a while, cooling off, when Tia strolls out. "Hey, that was so kick ass. Where the hell did you learn to dance like that?"

I grin. "I don't know. If you want something bad enough, you learn how. I thought it'd be fun, so I figured it out." I shrug and take a drink from the bottle. "It isn't as hard as it seems."

She nods and takes a drink from her own bottle. "Every time I think I'm in shape, I find out that I'm not. God, and no wonder why everyone is saying Granz is hot. He is a da-ahm fine piece of ass."

"Yeah, he's got a great ass."

I don't realize what time it is. I don't realize that anyone is behind me.

"Thanks, Colleli," Peter says, tossing me my stuff. It smacks me in the stomach, but I catch it. "And all this time I thought you were saying I was an ass. My mistake."

My face turns red and my eyes go wide. Peter doesn't stop walking. He keeps going, heading toward the parking lot. I shove Tia lightly. She's laughing at me. "You suck," I hiss. "You knew he was there."

"Yeah, I did. It was perfect. I had to."
She's laughing, guzzling water from her
bottle, nearly choking.

"I'll get you back. Just wait."

"Go ahead and try!" Tia yells, as I
sprint across the parking lot toward Peter's
car.

I duck inside, out of breathe. "I didn't
say that." I feel the need to clarify as I click
my seatbelt.

"I didn't hear anything, I mean, besides
the comment about my super-fine ass." He
laughs and looks over at me. "I can't figure
you out. You act like we're friends, and
that's it—then, you go and do stuff like
that. You're baffling."

"Baffling? No, I think you've got the
wrong word. I'm…" my eyes cut to Peter,
as he pulls out of the parking lot and onto
the road. I slump back into my seat and let
out a rush of air. "I don't know what I am.
A train wreck. A mess. Damaged goods.
Pick one. Or all three."

He shakes his head and smiles. "You're
a hot mess, an enigma, a poem—all raw
emotion with nothing held back."

I blurt out a laugh, because he couldn't be more wrong. "With nothing held back? I hold everything back."

"No, you don't. You're clear as crystal."

"You're insane."

"And that's how I know that I'm right. You do that a lot, you know?" I look at him. I have no idea what he's talking about. Apparently, he can tell that I don't follow. "You talk that way when I get too close to the truth. You get defensive and call me names. It means that I'm right."

"It could just mean that I think you're an ass, and nothing more." I'm about to say I told you so when Peter glances at me. From the look on his face, I can tell he's not going to let it drop.

"Are you attracted to me, Sidney?"

The question makes my stomach jump up my throat. I can't look at him. I feel my face getting hot, along with the rest of me. I manage to blurt out, "What the hell? Who asks that?"

"Uhm, I did. Are you attracted to me? It's a simple question." Peter glances at me, and then back at the road.

Thank God it's dark. I'm pretty sure my face has exploded into flames. I want to tell him that he's a bad, bad, man but that sounds too juvenile, so I say, "You're such a jerk!" I cover my face with my hand and look out the window. My pulse is roaring in my ears. I feel Peter's gaze slip over my neck for a moment. Why does he do this to me? So what if I think he's hot? It's not as though we can do anything. It doesn't matter. But still, I'd rather not say it.

"Well, that looks like a yes. Should I tell you what I think of you?"

"I don't care," I mumble, still looking out the window.

"Oh. Well, then I won't tell you." He's grinning, driving into the darkness to the restaurant on the other side of town.

I expect him to continue teasing me, but he doesn't say anything else. The silence spans between us and my mind latches onto the last thing he said. Now, I really want to know what he thinks of me. I can't believe he can sit there quietly and not tell me. I flick my eyes toward him. Peter is still driving with that infuriatingly sexy grin on his face, as if he knows exactly what he did.

I stare at the night sky and wonder why that question bothered me so much. Of course I'm attracted to him. Of course he already knows that. We nearly slept together. But that's not it. It's not what he knows that scares me. It's what he doesn't know. I'm attached to him. Given the choice to hang out with Peter or Millie, I'd choose Peter. He understands me better. He's become my best friend. It doesn't matter that he's my boss or my teacher. I feel comfortable around him. I've grown accustomed to his voice, his face. Every time Peter steps into the room, every time he swings me around in his arms, I feel peace—no it's beyond that—I feel happy. My stomach sinks as I wonder what that means.

I think I know.

I glance at Peter. I'm staring at the side of his face, drinking in the stubble along his jaw and the way his dark hair curls by his ears. His skin is so perfect, and his eyes— oh God—his eyes are like gemstones. When I look at them, it's as if I'm lost in a beautiful blue cavern covered in sparkling sapphires. And for once in my life, I feel safe. I don't worry about him hurting me, or touching me, or forcing me.

I don't realize how long I'm watching him until Peter turns and looks at me. He smiles softly and it feels like I'm in a free-fall. My stomach floats up to my mouth and I can't speak.

Oh no. No, no, no, no, no. My eyes are a little too wide when I look back out the windshield. My brain is chanting *no*, over and over again, as if it will erase the discovery my mind just made. My heart laughs. As if these things can be undone, as if it's possible to fall out of love as easily as it is to fall in love.

I love him? That can't be.

I deny it. That's not what's happening. It can't be. I don't love him. That's insane. I don't even know him.

But you do, that sweet reassuring voice says in the back of my head. I beat her with a broom and stuff her in a closet. She's usually the sane voice in my mind. I would have sworn that she is my reason, but that was not reasonable. I don't know Peter, not like that. I don't want to. I can't—

My frantic thoughts get cut off when Peter pulls into the parking lot. I'm panicking. Things aren't the same as they were two seconds ago. I realized that I have feelings for the guy sitting next to me. Maybe I'm dense as a dinosaur for not noticing—damn, everyone else noticed—but I don't know what to do now. Act the same? Pretend the thought never crossed my mind?

I take too long to get out of the car. Peter walks around to open my door.

"What are you doing?" I ask, as he offers his hand and pulls me up from my seat. Peter's looking down at me with those eyes. I forget to breathe.

He stands too close. I step away, and back into the car. Peter steps closer, closing the gap. He's close enough to touch me, but he doesn't. His eyes sweep over me before he asks, "Don't you want to know what I think?"

I shake my head slowly, careful to avoid his gaze, and tuck a piece of hair behind my ear. "No." My voice is too soft. Damn it. It sounds like a *yes*. I clear my throat and try again. I have to look up. I know I have to do it. Just say it. Spit it out as if it doesn't matter, because once he tells me what he thinks, I won't be able to let it go. I don't want things to change. What we have is good.

Looking directly into his eyes, I smile and say, "I don't want to know what you think. I don't feel that way about you." The lie burns my tongue.

He doesn't back away. Instead, Peter stays there, watching me. He leans close to my ear, and says, "I think you're beautiful, and that sharp tongue of yours…. God, I've never wanted to kiss a woman so much in my life. I will kiss you tonight. I won't be able to help myself." I shiver as he speaks. When Peter pulls away, my body is tense. My spine is stiff and my head is spinning like I'm falling down a rabbit hole.

"I don't know what to say." I'm watching him, barely breathing. My eyes are locked on his lips, wondering if he'll really do it.

Peter runs his hand along my cheek; his eyes are on my mouth. "Then, don't say anything." He turns and walks away. He's crossing the parking lot. I stand there, watching him head inside. When he pulls the door open, he looks back at me. "Coming, Colleli?"

Peter's screwing with me. He has to be messing with me. I blow off everything he just did and walk confidently across the parking lot. Screw him. Two can at play this game.

Peter's holding the door open. I turn to the side as I pass him, sucking in air. We're too close. I do it on purpose. My chest barely brushes against his as I pass. The sensation shoots way too many tingles through me, but I know he feels it, too. The way he stops breathing and looks up tells me that it was completely unexpected.

"Excuse me," I say, way too breathily, before stepping away. Peter's lips are parted. His shoulders are back, rigid. I turn toward the hostess station with a wicked grin. Peter is still sucking in air like he's been kicked in the stomach. "Table for two, please."

Peter suddenly moves and steps toward me. I feel the heat from his body against my back. He whispers in my ear, "That was evil."

"You started it," I say over my shoulder, smiling.

We follow the hostess to the same table we always sit at. It's our table. How did that happen? Peter steps in front of the girl and pulls out my chair and I sit down. The hostess stands there, waiting to hand us menus. Peter pushes me toward the table gently, and then takes his seat opposite me. His eyes glitter with mirth. He has a smug half grin on his face. For a brief second, his eyes drop to my lips. It makes me squirm in my chair. I can't believe he said that before. He was teasing me. He had to be.

"So," Peter says.

"So." My voice catches in my throat.

The way he's looking at me, as if he wants to kiss me until my knees give out and I fall into his arms, makes me flustered. I don't understand him. We've been hanging around each other since he arrived. Aside from the first night, Peter hasn't overtly done anything. Has he? I suddenly feel stupid. What if all the flirting was real? I assumed it wasn't. I thought he was teasing. Is Peter crazy enough to try and be with me, even if it costs him his job? He's a new teacher. That would be incredibly stupid, damning the rest of his career. So what is he thinking? I have no idea.

I start to open my mouth to tell him that we can't do anything like that—no kissing, no nothing—when I see her walk past the fireplace. Dr. Strictland's face lights up when she sees Peter. "Dr. Granz, Miss Colleli. What a pleasant surprise." She's wearing a rich crimson suit that makes her hair look Annie orange.

"Cyianna," Peter says, "how nice to see you. Won't you join us?"

She shakes her head. "No, I came in here to grab a dinner and go over some papers for my graduate students." She smiles at us and then looks at me. "I heard you were assisting the new dancing club."

"I am. We were just there. Dr. Granz is the sponsor."

She looks at both of us. "I see." She says it as though she really sees something. Strictland looks back at Peter. "You know what; I think I will join you. I've worked hard enough and it's been a long day." The hostess brings another chair and Dr. Strictland sits down next to me. She pats my knee and I nearly jump out of my seat. She gives me a funny look. "Sorry, dear."

"It's okay," I lie. I hate being touched. My gaze lifts. There's an exception to that rule. Peter somehow got around it. I smile nervously, wondering if we're going to get in trouble, but Strictland doesn't say anything about us being here together.

The meal progresses normally. We all know each other. The subject matter flips between the university, the department, classes, and then to literature.

Just when I think Strictland's not going to mention it, she does. "I hate to ruin a friendship or make things awkward between the two of you, but certain things have come to my attention."

Peter smiles and shakes his head, "Cyianna—"

"Peter, I know you well enough to realize that you won't do anything stupid. But you're young and Miss Colleli is younger. You both have roles to play, expectations to fulfill. Friendship is encouraged, but nothing more. I only see friendship here, and for both of your sakes, I hope it stays that way.

"Sidney, I don't need to remind you about your scholarship. The university will not pay you to retake classes due to sexual indiscretion." Oh my God. Did she just say that? My face burns. I manage to nod. "And Peter, you already know the severity of this. I hope I won't have to mention it again."

"You didn't have to mention it now," Peter says evenly.

Strictland watches him for a moment. She pats her napkin to her lips and places it on her plate. "You've been through more than most people, Peter. I consider myself a fair person. Let me be blunt. This arrangement that you have with your student looks wrong. You were dancing with her and then took her for dinner at one of the nicest establishments in town. According the hostess, they have seen the two of you here before—several times. Propriety has a look and this is not it. I don't want to see or hear about anything like this again. Consider this a polite warning, Dr. Granz. I apologize for ruining your evening, but it had to be stated." She stands, nods at us both, and then walks away.

CHAPTER 18

I glance at Peter, but he doesn't look back at me. The consequences have been spelled out. If we keep this up, we both lose everything. The lump in my throat feels like a sugar cube. It won't move. It's just stuck. I want to say something to Peter, make him smile again, but it's as though someone blew out the light in his eyes.

I can't stand the silence any more. "We're just friends, Peter. She knows that. So, we don't eat here anymore." I try to make light of it.

Peter looks up at me. His lips are parted, as though he can't believe what I just I said. "Don't lie to me, Sidney. I know you. This may be friendship, but there's more to it than that. Everyone can see it. I know you see it. I wish you'd admit it. At least, then we could decide what to do together." He pauses and then shakes his head when I don't say anything. "Are you so messed up that you don't even recognize your own feelings anymore?"

His words feel like a slap. I stiffen and look away.

I love him. I know I love him. Those words pierce my heart. My jaw twitches. I want to say it. I want to tell him that it's so much more than he thinks, but I'm afraid that he'll run. Maybe Peter's infatuated, but I'm not.

"You're damn right that I didn't want to admit it," I say. "And no, I don't have a good handle on my feelings anymore. For all practical purposes, the only emotion I've felt for the past four years has been pain. It never stops. Then, I met you." I'm breathing hard. I feel my chest rise as I speak. I can't stop the torrent of words flowing out of my mouth. "Things changed. Maybe I didn't recognize what I felt then, but I do now. I'm a stupid girl who fell in love with her friend, and that's not even the worst part. The worst part is that I'll lose everything if I tell you. This little patch of happiness will wither and die, and it will be all my fault, because I couldn't keep my mouth shut. I'd rather have you as a friend than not at all."

Peter's back is rigid, like someone replaced his spine with steel bar. Shocked, wide, eyes look back at me. He doesn't try to cut me off, and the more I talk, the worse he looks. By the time I finally shut up, Peter looks as if he's been hit on the side of the head with a board. The only response is a shocked blink.

Screw it. I'm not sitting here waiting for him to reject me. I jump up from the table and walk toward the ladies room. I feel tears building behind my eyes. I barely make it up the staircase and push open the door before big wet tears roll down my cheeks. Clutching the counter, I look up into the mirror. *Calm down.* I hear that little voice speaking softly inside my head.

"I ruined everything." I clutch my face and sob into my hands. I don't want to be alone. I need him, and telling Peter how I feel was the stupidest thing I could have done. Strictland said our friendship was over the line, so I tell him that I love him. What the hell is wrong with me?

I twist on the faucet and splash some water on my face. My crying slows, but my face still feels hot and puffy. When I go back downstairs, I need to act like I'm fine no matter how I feel inside. I need some fresh air, just for a second.

I walk over to the small window and yank the string for the blinds. They pull up quickly and I tug on the window, opening it. My vision is blurry and it's dark, so I don't notice until it's too late. There's a squirrel clinging to the outside of the window. When I throw it open, the little beast starts to slip. His nails are lodged into the wooden frame, but the rapid movement when I slide the window open knocks him loose. His nails screech as he slides down the glass.

I watch for a moment and realize that it can't get a grip. We're on the second floor. A strange impulse pounds through me. He's going to fall. It'll be my fault. I can't be a squirrel killer.

I shriek and stomp my feet—as if that will help—and shove my arms out the window to try and catch the little creature. The squirrel falls into my hands. My heart is about to explode. When the squirrel touches me, my brain shoots warning message and before I realize what I'm doing, I'm yanking my hands back inside. The squirrel clings to my arm.

I scream like someone is killing me and hop up and down, trying to get him to let go. When that doesn't work, I scream louder and spin in circles, whipping around as fast as I can, hoping the squirrel flies off. I only stop when he slides down my arm and his claws run out of skin to grab. I watch the animal sail across the room and smack into the wall.

At the same time that happens, the bathroom door flies open. Peter is standing there, ready to punch someone when a frightened squirrel darts between his legs. Peter glances down, surprised. He turns on his heel and watches it run down the hall. Screams erupt a moment later.

Peter looks up at me. I'm holding my clawed arm with my hand. My bottom lip quivers and sobs bubble up from inside of me. I can't stop crying. I feel so stupid, so incredibly foolish. Peter walks to me, smiling and pulls me into his arms. For a moment, he just holds me. His fingers tangle in my hair and he keeps me tightly nuzzled to his chest.

When Peter lets go, he looks down at my arm. The scratches aren't deep. "Did it bite you?" I shake my head and wipe the tears away. Peter is trying so hard not to smile. "What happened? Were you guys fighting over a stall?"

Tears are still in my eyes, but the smile on his face makes me smile, too. I thump my fist into his chest. "We weren't fighting over a stall! I opened the window to get some air. There was a squirrel. When I pulled the window open, I thought he was going to die, so I caught him… and then I freaked out a little bit."

Peter tries not to smile. He tries to keep a straight face and not laugh, but he's doing a terrible job. He takes my head between his hands and looks me in the eye.

"You're all right? No rabies? No serial killer squirrels hiding in one of the stalls?"

"Shut up. You would have screamed, too." I twist out of his grip and swipe at him.

Peter laughs, really laughs. It shakes his whole body and tears form in his eyes. He rubs the heel of his hand over his eyes and says, "I would have. No doubt."

"Then why are you laughing?" I'm pouting. I don't mean to, but I'm an emotional lunatic. We hear someone scream and then a crash. They still haven't caught the little beast. Damn squirrel.

"Because this is the kind of thing that would only happen to you. You're at the best restaurant in town and get attacked by a squirrel." He starts laughing again.

I fold my arms over my chest; the impulse to laugh with him is too strong. I smirk, saying, "When we retell it, let's just say it was a bear."

That makes him laugh harder. The two of us stand in the ladies room way too long, leaning into each other and laughing. By the time we go to leave, my ribs hurt from giggling so much.

The restaurant apologizes over and over again. They hate that I was attacked by a rodent in their bathroom. They comp our meal, and give us a ton of gift cards so we'll come back. The manager is worried that we'll tell everyone that they have animal problems, even though I have no intention of mentioning this to anyone for as long as I live.

Peter and I return to his car. On the way back to the dorm, he asks me if I have stuff to take care of my cuts. I don't.

"I have a first aid kit at my place. Let's patch you up and then I'll take you home."

"Your place?" I ask, and glance over at him. He still hasn't said anything about my, *I fell in love with my best friend* thing. I'm hoping he'll never mention it again. I feel stupid enough as it is. I tease, "You're not asking me up for coffee again, are you?"

He laughs. "No, but you can't leave that cut untreated. You'll grow a tail or something. Besides, it's on the way to your dorm."

I nod. I go to his place. I don't realize what will happen. I don't realize any of it.

CHAPTER 19

"The scrape looks superficial," Peter says, holding my arm and examining the cuts gently. There are nine angry red pin-sized scrapes down one arm. We are sitting in his bathroom. The medicine cabinet is open. It's the first time I've been in his house since the night I met him. Everything is put away now. Peter is very neat. I'm shocked that he even has a kit like this.

I still feel silly. Who gets attacked by small wildlife creatures? I'm the antithesis of Snow White. "It probably wouldn't have happened if I didn't scream like a lunatic and launch the squirrel at the wall. I freaked out on his little ass."

Peter is grinning when looks up at me. "Yes, you did. I heard you yelling in the dining room. By the time I threw the door open, I was sure someone was killing you. Then, I see you launch a small animal across the room." He laughs. "I have the shower scene from Psycho in my head, except Norman Bates is a squirrel. You better watch your step. When he gets out of that restaurant, he's gonna tell all his buddies." Peter's shoulders are shaking. He's trying so hard not to laugh.

I'm grinning. Norman the Squirrel with his little knife is kind of funny. "Jerk."

"Hold still. Odds are this'll sting like a bitch."

"Do bitches really stin—" I stop asking stupid questions and let out a slew of swear words. "What the hell is that? Acid?" I rip my arm away. My skin burns as if he set it on fire.

Peter reaches for my hand and yanks it back out. "Baby." He holds a bottle of stuff over my arm again. There's a towel under my elbow. The liquid runs down my arm and onto the towel.

Peter pours it quickly, again. My body tenses and I grit my teeth. I'm ready for it this time. My jaw locks, but I nearly fall over when Peter lowers his head and blows on the bubbling cuts. His pink lips are pursed and he blows on my skin. The gentle rush of air chases away the sharp burn and makes my skin cold. I forget to lock my jaw. I'm still tense, but the reason has changed. Peter doesn't seem to realize what he's done. He's still grinning and looks up at me.

No, no, no. I have a deer in the headlights look on my face. I don't move. I can't think. I can't breathe. Peter's eyes darken. He doesn't look away. My heart pounds louder. I think he can hear it. Suddenly, I notice my breathing, the way I'm taking shallow shaky breaths. Peter's fingers remain on my wrist, holding my arm out across my knee. I'm lost in his gaze. I feel a magnetic pull toward him, towards his lips. My skin is charged from his touch. I can't stand it. Sucking in air, I turn my face.

I can't do it.

I can't kiss him.

I shouldn't even be here.

Peter's voice is deeper than usual. "That should help. Let me get the antiseptic, and cover it up. Then, we can take you home." He drops my wrist and stands up. Peter is staring at the little bottle, but he doesn't take it in his hands. Instead, he stands there, unblinking. He breathes in deeply and lets the air rush out from between his lips. I feel like I'm watching porn. My pulse is racing and I'm too warm. I can't look away. I don't want to.

Peter runs his hands through his hair and grabs the ointment. "Here, this should help it heal faster." He dabs it on my arm. My stomach curls at his light touch. I watch Peter as he presses his finger to the scrapes. It makes me shiver so badly that I yank my arm away.

Peter looks up at me. My mouth is open, but I have no words. What am I supposed to say? *Your touch makes me crazy? Every time you dab that stuff on me, I tingle in all the wrong places?* What the hell is wrong with me?

I jump off the little bench in the bathroom and try to push past him. Peter turns at the last second. Our bodies line up. Ice drips down my spine and I freeze. His pecs are lined up with mine. I can feel him. It sends shivers through me that turn into a throb. My lips part and I gasp, trying to say words that won't come. I try to move my feet. I try to do anything but stay there and look up into his eyes.

Peter lifts his hands slowly. I feel the heat from his palms just below my elbows. I know he wants to touch me. I know what he's debating, because the same thoughts are racing through my mind. I know I should I move, but I can't. My pulse pounds harder, roaring in my ears. I feel his hands nearly touch the bare skin on my arms. Peter's hands are so close, but they don't touch me.

I don't lift my gaze, even though I feel Peter's eyes burning a path from my eyes to my lips. If I look up, I won't be able to leave. If I look up, I'll throw everything away. Throwing away college means going home. It means going back to the people I ran away from. It means seeing the man who used my body over and over again.

My voice is so strained when I speak. "I can't…"

Peter's face is so close. He's lowered his head. I can feel his breath on my lips. My fingers ball at my sides. I stretch my hands and then curl my fingers into fists.

Don't touch him. Don't.

"I know," Peter breathes. I close my eyes and feel the room tip to the side. *It's so hot in here.* He's so close to me. I peel my eyes open again, and stare at his chest. I won't look up. I can't look up. "We can't, but I can't let you go."

My eyes flick up. Oh, God. Mistake. Sirens are ringing in my ears. I fall into those twin pools of pure blue and I can't climb out. I gasp. My lips are right by his. Peter's hands are still over my arms. Every few moments, his fingers clench shut, as though he's fighting the urge to touch me. I try to swallow. I try to look down, but I'm so hopelessly tangled in his gaze. I want his hands on me. I want to feel his palms burning on my skin. I want things that I thought I'd never want.

My lips are parted. I try to speak, but nothing comes out. Every breath I take swells inside me, forcing my chest out, making my breasts brush against his chest. I need to stop breathing. My head is swimming with lust. Part of me is begging to be touched, to be kissed. I can't stop it. I can't control it. I'm trapped.

Peter's hands unclench and he closes his eyes. When he opens them again, there's a hopeless smile on his face. He starts talking, pouring his heart out, every last damaged bit. "I'm never the lucky one. Every time I find someone, she gets ripped away. She's always out of reach and it's not like I can change that.

"I can't get her back. I can't change things. There are no second chances. I've lost everything. I lost Gina.

"I lost myself when she died. I haven't felt a goddamn thing since then. But then you came along... You're smart and beautiful. I thought I could move on, but I couldn't. I wasn't ready. You were the only person who understood that, and knew what it truly meant.

"And now," Peter laughs bitterly and presses his eyes closed. When he opens them again, he looks tormented. His voice becomes higher as he speaks. His words come faster, more pained, more panicked. "Now that I'm ready to move on, I can't. I can't lose my job. I can't be with you, but I can't be without you. God, Sidney. Tonight was one of the best and worst moments of my life. You said you loved me. *You love me...*" he smiles sadly and shakes his head. "I love you, too. You brought me back to life. You gave me back my smile. You're everything to me, but I can't do this to you—"

I stare at him. My eyes are too wide and my mouth is hanging open. What did he say? He can't mean that. He can't, but he said it. *Peter loves me.* But I can't follow him. There's so much agony in his voice. I don't know what he means. "Do what to me?"

"You're here on scholarship. I know what will happen to me if I go through with this, and I can't let you throw away your life—"

He loves me. I stare at his eyes, listening to him say it, listening to the reason why he's frozen, why he's not touching me. He loves me.

I'm so afraid, so terrified that he'll push me away, but I do it anyway. For a split second, I'm brave—and stupid, and reckless and impulsive. I cut off his words by slipping my fingers over his stubbled cheeks. I lean in and brush my lips to his. His mouth is sweet and soft.

Peter freezes when I kiss him. His arms don't wrap around me. He doesn't kiss me back. My muscles are so tense, so ready to run. I thought he'd hold me. I thought he'd respond.

Shame floods my face. I break the tiny kiss and look down. "I'm sorry," I say to the floor. "I shouldn't have done that. I shouldn't have…" My lower lip is quivering. I try to hold it still, but it won't cooperate, so I suck my lip into my mouth and bite down.

Before I can say another word, Peter scoops me up into his arms. I yelp and hold on tight. He walks us to the front door and lowers me to the floor. My body slides against his. The hem of my dress slips up shamefully high as I get down and press my feet to the floor. He's going to throw me out again. My hands are on his chest.

Peter doesn't step away. I feel his eyes on my face. I can't let go. He lets out a breath and leans into me. His hands are on my shoulders. He looks at my fingers on his chest. "I can't tell you to go."

"Then don't."

"I can't sleep with you."

"Then we won't."

He laughs at that. "You make it sound easy. I can barely think with you touching me like that. You seriously think I have enough self-control not to sleep with you?"

I nod. My fingers are splayed over his chest. I feel all of him, every curve, every muscle. "Your headlights are on." My thumb rubs over his pec, feeling the taut nipple beneath.

He laughs, and says, "So are yours," right before my thumb moves over him. He moans and grabs my hand. "Sidney."

"Peter."

"You're too— You don't know what you're giving up." His voice is husky. The muscles in his neck are flexed tight. He keeps clenching his jaw and smashing his lips together.

"I know exactly what I'm giving up. I remember who's waiting for me at home." My hands slide down his chest. His abs are so ripped. My finger flicks a button on his shirt, just above his waist.

Peter's shoulders tense. He lets out a ragged breath. Peter's hand lifts and brushes my cheek. I lean into the touch and close my eyes. He pulls away from me like I burned him. "Sidney, I can't do this. I can't." Peter pulls at his hair and turns away from me. He paces the floor once, then twice.

When he looks up, I panic. I see it in his eyes. He's going to push me away. I don't move. I brace for impact, expecting him to open the door and throw me through it, but he doesn't. He rushes toward me and places hands on either side of my head. I don't know what he's doing. I can't tell if he's going to yell or—

I don't get to finish the thought. Peter leans in. His lips are so close to mine. I feel him resist. That part of him is still fighting it, but he doesn't back away. Peter closes the space. His lips press lightly to mine. It's a whisper of a kiss. Peter's still holding back. His body is all taut muscle. When I lift my hands and try to touch him, Peter jumps and pulls away. His face is scrunched with indecision. His hands fist at his sides. He looks like he wants to hit the wall, and turns away from me.

I'm insane. I walk over to him. I'm behind him. I made up my mind. I can't do this to him. It's tearing him apart. I feel the strength I need to walk away. It's faint, but it's there. "Peter, it's okay. I'm sorry. I won't do this to you."

His face is in his hand. Peter turns around slowly and looks down at me. "I can't do this to you. I know what you went through to get here. I can't send you back to the people who did that to you... I can't let you do it. I love you, Sidney." His eyes search mine. It feels as though we're breaking up. Something tightens around my throat. I try to swallow, but I can't.

"I love you, too, Peter." I smile at him sadly and turn to leave.

My hand is twisting the knob when he says, "Stay."

"What?"

"Stay, just a little longer. I can't let you go, not yet."

I'm near tears. After everything we've been through, I can't believe I have to walk away from him. Life is so unfair, this is so wrong. I love him and he loves me. The odds are so slim, so miniscule, that a person will find their match. I know he was made for me, and I know I have to leave.

I shake my head. "I can't. This is an all or nothing kind of deal. I can't stand being around you and not touching you. You asked me if I'm attracted to you—I am. A lot. Everything about you entices me. Peter, I need to go." Pressing my lips together, I walk out of his apartment and fly down the steps. I suck in the night air like I'm suffocating. I walk the two blocks to my dorm, alone, thinking.

I'd give up everything for him, but then what? He has no job, I have no money, and we both live in a box.

Love sucks.

CHAPTER 20

I feel hollowed out. Even my skin feels fragile. My fingers drift to my lips. The memory is still there. It's like I can still feel the pressure of Peter's mouth, the way he fit perfectly into the seam of my lips.

I can't see Peter again. That doesn't really sink in until I'm walking down the street. There's a good chance that I won't even be his TA anymore. Strictland will separate us.

I think about how my days will be without Peter, having him so close but not being able to talk to him, or touch him. Oh God, it hurts. It feels like someone took a knife and carved out my heart. I want to double over and cry, but I don't. I keep walking.

A car full of guys slows as they drive by. They whistle and catcall me before zooming off. When I'm finally on campus again, I'm back in my element. I can handle this. I make a beeline for the dorm. When I get to my room, it's filled with girls. God, why can't I ever be alone? Millie looks at me over the tops of several ponytails. They've got a vat of blue Kool-Aide and are dipping the ends of their hair into the tub. Tia is sitting by the door. Her arms are folded over her chest and she's leaning back in a chair.

"Not into blue?" I ask.

She shakes her head. "Nah, I'd love blue, but the only way it'll show up in my hair is if I bleach it first. I'm not bleaching it. It'd probably fall out or something." She glances up at me, and notices my puffy eyes. "What's up with you? Something happen?"

I nod. "Yeah, the normal shit. Got chewed out by Strictland for being Peter's friend, and got attacked by a squirrel. The damn thing ripped my arm off." Tia looks at my face to see if I'm making stuff up and then back at my arm.

"Holy shit. You're serious?" she asks, and sits up straight. I nod. Before I can say anything else, she's up and tugging me out of the room and down the hall. "Millie's blonde and going to stick her whole head in that bucket. It's going to take her all night to get the color to show up. So talk. What's going on with you? Why'd Strictland chew you out?" She pauses and her eyes widen. "Shit, Peter? As in Dr. Peter Granz?" I nod. She pulls me into her room and closes the door. "My roommate is down there with Millie. Spill. What the hell is going on?"

I flop down on her bed with my shoulders slumped forward. I shrug. "I don't even know. Peter is Dr. Granz. It's a long story, but I nearly slept with him before I realized who he was."

Tia's eyes bug out of her head. "What?"

"Millie dragged me out on a blind date when she wanted to hook up with Brent. I was supposed to meet them there. Long story short, I sat down at the wrong table."

I look up at her face. Tia is really nice. I've said stupid crap to her before, but this makes me nervous. "Don't tell anyone, okay? I don't want him to get in trouble."

"I'm not telling anyone, but you have to tell me what happened. How'd you end up with him that night if you were on a date with another guy?"

"The other guy had happy hands. I left early. When I went to the parking lot, Peter was standing there with his hood up. He was new here and alone. Plus he's hot and funny. I don't know. I ended up going home with him. We made out. A lot. Before things got out of hand, the phone rang and I left. I recognized him the next morning in class."

"Holy shit!" she stomps her feet on the floor, way too excited. "So, what now?"

"We grabbed dinner after club. It was nothing, but Strictland showed up and ate with us. Then she kinda gave an ultimatum. Peter gets fired and trashes his career if he continues to see me, and I get flunked and can't graduate. I can't repeat classes because of the scholarship. And I have no money. She knows that."

Tia is at the edge of her seat with her fingers by her mouth. "Oh, my God. But wait, I thought you said nothing was going on?"

"Nothing was going on. We were friends with an awkward start, but…" I sigh and tug at my hair.

"But it's more than that now?"

"Yeah, way more. Holy fuck, Tia. Like holy frickin' fuck. I can't even tell you." My lips mash together. I want to punch something. "It's not like I've been cut off from my best friend, although he is and I have been—it's worse than that. I feel like my heart got ripped out.

"And Peter. We were at his apartment fixing this," I point to the claw marks, "and I kissed him. He said he can't, but he loves me—"

Tia gasps, "Oh, my God. Do you love him?" I glance up at her. She tenses and shakes the bed with her hands and squeals when I don't answer. It must be written all over my face because she says, "Oh, my God! That's so romantic! You love him, but you can't be with him. What are you going to do?"

I shrug. "Nothing. There's nothing to do. I can't let him risk his career for me, and I have to graduate. I can't fuck it up and go home." I bury my face in my hands and rub hard. Everything is falling apart. I feel so fractured, like I'm crumbling.

"I've never heard you curse like that before."

"There's not been much to curse about. I have no idea what to do. I have to stay away from him, but I can't." I laugh bitterly and wrap my arms around my waist. I can't chase away the sensations that are choking me. I'm looking at her floor.

Memories well up, uncalled. "That was my first *I love you*, well, the first one that was real, and then this happens. We aren't even friends anymore. We can't be. I have no idea how to deal with this." My hands are on the sides of my head, and I shove my fingers into my hair.

Tonight started out great. I can't believe this is happening. Yes, I should have known, but I didn't. I didn't know I was falling in love with Peter. I didn't even realize it until tonight. I'm so damned stupid. How did I not see it? Especially when everyone has been less than tactful about it.

"Oh, God," I groan into my hands. Looking up, I ask, "What do I do?"

Tia's face is full of sympathy. "The only thing you can do. Stay away from him and distract yourself with chocolate."

CHAPTER 21

The next few weeks pass painfully slow. At night I stare at the ceiling. I can't sleep. It feels like my arms have been chopped off. I have phantom pains. God, and the nightmares. My mind drifts and I see Peter getting hit by a car, falling off a cliff, or getting shot in the chest. Every time it's the same—I see what's going to happen moments before it occurs. I run toward Peter, screaming at the top of my lungs, but he doesn't hear me. I'm never fast enough, never loud enough, and I'm always a second too late. There are never any good-byes; Peter's simply ripped away from me.

One night the dream is so vivid. Peter is smiling, saying something to me. He's stepping backward with that wry grin on his face. The ground is hard and dry. The clay cracks, but Peter doesn't look behind him. The parking lot turns into nothing but miles and miles of cracked red clay. It's like watching him walk onto thin ice. I'm frantic, calling to him—begging him to come back—but he can't hear me. The ground under his feet suddenly cracks apart. Peter falls. I launch myself toward him, toward the massive chasm in the ground. I fall at the edge of the hole just in time to have Peter's fingers narrowly miss mine.

I scream.

I shriek so loudly that the nightmare becomes real. I yell in my bed and dart upright. My body is covered in cold sweat. The sheets are stuck to my body. I'm tangled and thrashing, trying to get free. Millie jumps up and flips on the lights. My hand is on my chest. I'm trying to tell myself that it wasn't real, that Peter is alive and well, but the dream feels so genuine that I'm close to tears.

Millie's standing there with a broom in her fists, as though she's going to bludgeon an intruder. When she sees that no one is around, her arms drop to her sides. "Are you all right?" She rubs her eyes and takes a deep breath.

I nod, but it's shaky. I can't speak. What am I afraid of? The nightmare sounds so stupid. The ground doesn't just eat people, but the dream felt real. I can't shake the feeling. I yank my blankets off and head to my closet. I pull out sweats and put them on.

Millie is watching me. "Where are you going? It's 4:00am. You can't go running now."

"I have to." It's all I can manage to huff out.

"Sidney, wait. I'll go with you." Millie's eyelids are about halfway open. She looks like she's falling asleep.

"It's fine. I'm okay. Go back to bed."

"I can't. Something's bothering you and I've turned into a shitty friend since Brent came along. Give me a second. I'll go with you." She blinks slowly and turns toward her closet. I'm already dressed and pulling on my sneakers.

When I tie the second shoe, I say, "I'd rather go alone. Seriously, go back to bed. I'll take your pepper spray if you're worried."

She yawns. Millie has one leg in her sweats and looks up at me. "Fine, but only if you use the student gym. Don't run outside. Go use the stair climber or elliptical or something. Promise?"

I nod. "Yeah. I'll see you at lunch."

And I'm gone. I run down the stairs and outside into the cold air. It fills my lungs and reminds me what's real and what's not. The dreams aren't real. Peter is alive. I know what the nightmares signify, I know what they mean. Peter was ripped away from me and there's nothing that I could have done about it. He's gone. It's as if he's dead, but I see his ghost haunting the English building every day.

Strictland removed me as his TA the day after she saw us at dinner. She swapped her TA with his. Now, I work with

Strictland. The rumors have stopped. No one is saying anything anymore.

I pound my feet harder and run faster. My lungs burn like I can't get enough air. My hair swishes back and forth, tickling my neck. I want to run so hard that my body screams in pain. I want to feel something that I know how to deal with, because I don't know what to do with this.

It's not the same as the other nightmares. Those had me scared to death, because someone was trying to hurt me. These dreams are the opposite. No one is hurting me, but it feels like my guts are being ripped out. It's like losing Peter all over again, night after night. When will it stop? The man is still alive. Why is my brain mourning him as if he were dead? I can't stand it. I want to scream.

Digging in, I push off the ground harder and run faster. I lengthen my stride. My arms pump at my sides and I sprint as fast as I can across campus to the far side where the new gym is located. By the time I get there, I can't breathe and there's a stitch running up both sides of my ribcage and across my hip.

I swipe my ID card and go inside. Holding my hands on my hips, I stop and suck in air. I stay like that for a few moments in the darkened hallway, just trying to catch my breath.

When the cramp subsides, I walk down to the exercise room. I don't expect anyone to be here. The halls are empty and the lights are off. I swipe my card and go inside. I find a treadmill and turn it on, increasing the speed up to a full run. I pound the crap out of the thing, sprinting as fast as I can.

A few moments pass and I'm in my own little world. Thoughts float away. The only thing in my head is the pounding of my heart and the rush of air filling my lungs. That's why he scares the shit out of me.

"Sidney?" Mark's voice comes from somewhere beside me. I yelp, lose my footing, and step on my sneaker. The result is instantaneous. I fall and get launched off the end of the treadmill. My back slams into the wall. "Holy shit!" Mark pulls out the emergency stop key and the treadmill turns off, before my feet get sucked under the thing. Then, he falls on his knees next to me. "Sidney, I'm so sorry. Are you all right? Can you move?"

I start laughing. It's the crazy kind of chuckling that makes people really uncomfortable, but I can't stop. Mark is still kneeling next to me. He glances around. "Awh shit. I broke her." He runs his hand through his hair and pokes my shoulder. "You okay, there? You sound a little bit nuts."

I take a deep breath and look over at him. "I am a little bit nuts. Why else would I be here at four in the morning. I assume you're twisted too, since you were sitting in here in the dark."

Mark looks offended. "I was not! I was back in the weight room when I heard someone. I came out to see who it was, said your name, made you fall on your ass, and then get battered by the wall."

I laugh and realize that I do sound way past crazy—and way past tired. I rub my hands over my face and sigh. "It's not the weirdest thing that's ever happened." When I pull my hand away, there's a streak of blood. "Damn it. I cut my face?"

Mark stands and offers his hand. I put my clean hand in his palm and he pulls me up. "Nah, it's just a little scrape on your cheek."

I dab it again with my fingers and walk over the mirrors. It's not that bad, but I look like hell. My hair is a rat's nest pulled into a ponytail. It's all bushy. I didn't bother brushing it before I left. I just pulled it back and snapped the elastic ring around my hair. There are dark circles under my eyes and I look beat.

Mark hands me a hanky. I look over at him, surprised. "It's not used, if that's what you're thinking."

I take it and say, "Thanks, and that wasn't what I was thinking at all." I take the white cotton and run it under the water fountain, getting it damp, and then blot my cheek. "I don't even know what did this."

He points to my wrist. "Your watch. Your hands tried to cover your face when you fell. The watch probably scratched you." I look at my wrist and then back up at him.

"So, what's your story?" I ask. I don't want him staring at me, but he is. I glance at him. "Are you always in here at four in the morning?"

Mark puts his hands behind his back and shakes his head. "Nah, it's usually five by the time I get here. I was early today. As to the reason why, well, I'm a bit of a freak. I only need four hours of sleep."

I'm dabbing my cheek as he's talking. When says that, I look up at him, envious. "Are you serious?"

"Yeah, it's some kind of genetic thing. My mom's like that. They thought it was ADHD for a long time, but that's not it. I just don't need to sleep eight hours to feel good. Four or five, max, and I'm good to go. I can stay out all night and then wake up at the butt crack of dawn.

"Since there's nothing to do at the dorm, and my roommate kills me if I wake him up, I usually head over here." He's leaning against the wall, watching me. Mark's closer to my age than Peter. This is the kind of guy I should be with. He's normal, nice, and my peer. He's not my teacher.

I watch Mark for too long, staring at his face, wondering what he would have done if I threw myself at him at the beginning of the semester—if it was Mark at the table and not Peter. Would he have done as much? Would he have stopped? What would that have done to me? Sometimes I think sex will fix everything. It ruined everything, so it makes sense, sort of.

I don't realize how much time has passed.

Mark gets a nervous smile on his face and looks around, like I must be watching something else. "Uhm, Sidney? Did I accidentally put you to sleep with my overly boring story?"

I smirk and blink. I hurt so much and he's so sweet. "No. You're anything but boring."

He grins. "You really think so?"

I nod. "I would have followed you around like a puppy if some other guy hadn't caught my attention first."

"Story of my life." Mark's eyes search my face before he lifts his hand and lightly touches my arm. It's a reassuring touch. "I'm guessing said guy is the reason you're here at this ungodly hour?"

I nod slowly. My thoughts are jumbled. I don't know what I want. I don't know how to make the agony inside of me stop. I'm staring at Mark's lips. I'm reverting. I can feel my old pre-Peter plan jumping around my ankles, nipping at me.

Mark is shirtless. His body is covered in a thin layer of sweat. His hair is damp and messy. I'm aware of my breathing, aware of his mouth, and aware that I'm standing too close to him. Mark's hand slips up my bare arm, over my shoulder, and touches my cheek.

He tucks a piece of my crazy hair behind my ear and smiles sadly at me. "I'm not a rebound guy, Sidney. I'm a love-her-with-my-whole-heart kind of guy, and since I really like you, it's so damn hard not to kiss you right now. But, I can't..." He breaks our gaze by looking down. Mark takes my hands and rubs his thumbs over my skin slowly. Breathing deeply, he adds, "Forgive me?"

Normally, I would have turned beat red, but today I just nod and look at our hands. "Then, how do you get over a broken heart? Everyone says sex, but I just don't…" I sigh deeply and look up at him.

"Since I've had mine stomped on a few times, I can tell you the truth." He tilts his head to the side and smiles at me. His eyes don't meet mine again, not while he's talking. "You don't get over it. Nothing immediately heals the pain. It doesn't vanish because you're ready to get over him. It takes time. One day, things won't hurt so much. One day you'll notice someone else and not think about the last guy at all. You'll be ready to start over, and so will your heart. Give it time, Sidney."

I nod and he pulls his hands away. "Why are you so nice to me?"

"Isn't it obvious?" I shake my head. "You're hot, like amazingly bodacious. I have a little crush on you." Mark looks sheepish when he says the last one.

I smile at him. My face feels funny and I realize that I haven't smiled in a while. "I didn't know."

"Yeah, well, I tend to keep things low key." He gives me a lop-sided grin and bumps me with his shoulder. "Want to race or something? I'm guessing you came in here to run and I bet I can totally beat you."

I glance out the windows at the track and nod. "Sounds good."

I spend the next hour running with Mark. We race until my muscles are twitching like I've been electrocuted. I fall onto the mats and lay on my back. Mark sits next to me in a comfortable silence. It seems that I've found another friend.

CHAPTER 22

I still have to see Peter once a week. I didn't get transferred out of his night class, although I wish I did. My only option would have been to drop it, and if I did that, I wouldn't be able to retake it because of my scholarship. It was too far into the semester by the time Strictland separated us. I'm just glad she didn't force me to drop it.

Peter's at the front of the room. I don't look at him. Instead, I hear his voice and stare down at my notepad. I've been up for a really long time. It seems like yesterday that I was sitting with Mark, but that was only this morning. I touch my face and feel the cut on my cheek. Yup, that was today. I can't believe I fell off a treadmill. Who does that?

"Miss Colleli?" Peter says. I get the feeling that it's not the first time he's called on me.

I look up. Everyone is watching me. "Sorry, what was that?"

Peter's eyes drift to the cut on my cheek. His brows pinch together. "The poem at the beginning of the book…" When I don't answer, he adds, "*The Man Who Was Thursday* had a poem at the beginning. What did you think it was about? Did it fit the literature?" Peter is standing in front of me for a moment. Then he crosses the room, leans back on his desk, and folds his arms across his perfect chest.

Why is he calling on me? I want to crawl into a hole and die. That's the one question that I can't answer at all. "It made me want buy a top hat," I say, and shrug. A few students giggle. One says *freak*. I turn and give that guy a thumbs-up. I'm a proud freak. Deal with it.

Peter stares at me with a hopeless look on his face. He doesn't ask me to elaborate. Instead he calls on the smartass who says he's not gay enough to think the poem is about hats. Peter pinches the bridge of his nose and looks at the clock. It's almost nine.

"Since no one knows what the hell the poem is about, you guys are going to hand in a research paper next week. I want three sources, four pages, double-spaced, and include your own understanding of the poem. If you agree with the research, state why. Class dismissed." They all groan and exit quickly.

I'm moving at slug speed. I feel so tired. I can't remember if I ate today. I don't think I did. I consider getting some food as I gather my books. By the time I head for the door, the classroom is empty, save Peter, who's at his desk.

"What happened to your face, Colleli?"

I raise my eyebrow and look back at him. "That's hardly complimentary, Dr. Granz." I do the shame, shame, thing with my fingers, too, but it's sloppy.

He gets up and walks toward me. "What's with you? You realize that your grades are so borderline that you might fail, right? And, with Strictland breathing down my neck, I can't pass you if you don't earn it."

I didn't realize that. My spine stiffens. "I don't want you to pass me through."

"Then, what the hell are you doing? I don't understand you. You wanted to take this class, didn't you?"

"I wanted to take it when Tadwick was teaching it." Peter flinches. Maybe I said that a little too harshly. "I didn't mean—"

Peter puts up his hands, palms toward me, and backs away. "I know what you meant. It's fine." He grips the back of his neck and sighs.

I've avoided looking at Peter's face, but when he's turned to the side—away from me—I chance it. His lashes are lowered, and his shoulders slumped like he's beaten, as if the weight was too much and it broke him. There are dark rings under his eyes that match mine. His lips no longer smile. Peter looks exhausted, with a sadness that penetrates every ounce of his being. He's drowning in melancholy.

Peter must feel my eyes on the side of his face, because he looks up. Our eyes meet and I wish they hadn't. My stomach drops to my feet. I'm dying. There was air and now there is none. Weeks have passed, but I'm not over him.

Peter breaks our gaze and looks down. "I better get going." His voice is faint, weak.

Before I know what I'm saying, the words are out of my mouth. "Do you regret it?" Peter looks up at me. His eyes slip over my face until he finds my eyes. "Because I do. I regret it so badly. If I could go back and undo everything, I would. I can't stand seeing you like this, and I can't stand being like this. If I never sat at your table—"

Peter talks over me. "If you never sat at my table, I would have never known that I could be happy again. No, I don't regret it. I don't regret any of it." He works his jaw, as if he wants to say more, but decides against it.

I nod slowly and pick up my books, not planning on saying anything else. A letter falls out of the pages and lands at Peter's feet. He bends over and picks it up. His eyes lift to mine. "Is this from your brother?" I nod. "I thought you were going to throw it out?"

"I did. He sent another and then another."

"You haven't opened any of them?"

I shake my head. "No," my voice is barely there. "He's dead to me. Take it. Toss it. I don't want to see it again."

I head toward the door. I feel Peter's eyes on my back. I know he wants to say something, but I don't give him the chance. I walk out of the room and down the hall. I exit at the front staircase. No one uses the stairs. There are over a hundred steps to the lawn below. I press my back to a pillar and slip down to the floor.

For a long time, I sit there in darkness. The lights around me illuminate the steps, but I'm in shadow. The people below can't see me.

I'm worried that Sam keeps sending me letters. When we were children, he and I were best friends. He looked out for me, took care of me. Sam let me play with his friends. He punched anyone that messed with me. I was his little sister even though we're twins. *You were born after me,* he'd say. *That's why you're my little sister.* I think he liked being the older brother. It made Sam feel important.

But all that changed when I cried to him about Dean. I expected him to defend me. He didn't. Sam said I was a tease, and that he'd seen what I did, the way I acted around his friend. The memories bubble up one by one. Once they start, they don't stop.

Dean didn't hurt you, they said. Dean is a good young man. I swear, it's as though my parents and Sam are standing in front of me, saying the same things over and over again. I want to cry out, *What about me?* He held me down, he overpowered me. Dean wouldn't do that, they said. God, I'd never felt so betrayed in my life.

But it was worse, so much worse when I told Sam.

I never let these memories out their box. They're like demons and will strip away every ounce of joy I have until there's nothing left. But I let the memories out. I hear their voices. The old words reopen scars that never healed. My mind is reeling. I need to force the demons back, and make it stop. I pull my knees into my chest and lower my head. Wrapping my arms around my ankles, I pull myself into a ball. I close my eyes, hoping that it'll pass or swallow me whole.

The door behind me opens. I hear it, but I don't look up. Whoever it is will just go down the staircase without even seeing me. The sound of footfalls comes nearer and then stops. I glance around my arm and see leather saddle shoes. I glance up at Peter.

He sits next to me. I tuck my face into my knees again. I don't want to talk to him.

"You look miserable."

"I am miserable." I talk into my knees.

"So am I." Peter takes a deep breath and puts his hand on my back. Peter pulls me to him and I wrap my hands around his waist. I hold onto him tightly, knowing that I'll have to let go. When he pulls away it feels like someone is ripping off my skin, layer by layer.

I push up and turn toward the stairs. "I can't do this, Peter. I can't be around you like this. It's killing me. I have no idea how to get over you. I just can't…" I step away, but he grabs my arm. I stiffen. I love it and I hate it. I want his arms around me. I want my friend back.

"I need to tell you something." He pulls me closer and takes my books away. He drops them on the ground next to his feet. His hands cup my cheeks. I feel Peter's breath on my face. It makes my head feel so light, dizzy almost. I want Peter's lips on mine. I miss him so badly that tears prick my eyes.

I take Peter's hands in mine and try to pull his hands down. "Don't, Peter… I can't do this." I'm barely in one piece. I feel the wave of regret growing bigger and bigger. It's going to crush me. His touch is going to destroy me. I panic. I pull at him but he doesn't let go. I'm crying. I didn't realize it, but tears are streaking my cheeks.

Peter's thumbs swipe through the tears on my cheeks, wiping them away. "Don't cry." He leans in and brushes his lips to my face, kissing away a tear. I still. My fingers are still clutching his hands, but I stop pulling. I take a ragged breath when he does it again, and again. Peter kisses my face lightly, brushing away every tear.

Then, he tilts my head back so that I can see his eyes. "I hope you can forgive me, but I did something incredibly stupid." The corner of his mouth lifts. Uncertainty lines his gaze. "I wrote a letter of resignation and put it on Strictland's desk.

"I can't do this anymore. Every time I see you, it's like I've had my heart ripped out of my chest. I can't eat, I can't sleep. It's not a crush. It was never a crush. I love you, Sidney. I took too long to say it. I took too long to fix this, but I choose you."

My jaw drops. "You quit?" He nods. My eyebrows creep up my face. Shocked silence encases me. When I finally try to speak, a loud sobbish-sounding laugh comes out of my mouth. I throw my arms around his neck and hold on tight. Peter presses his body against mine and lifts me off my feet. He swings me around once. I shriek and laugh. "But, you can't do that!"

When Peter puts me down, he's smiling. "I already did. I wrote a letter of resignation and slipped it under her door." I turn to go inside. I have to get that letter back. I'm so happy he chose me, but I can't let him do this.

When I try to go inside, Peter reaches for me. His fingers wrap around my arm. Ice shoots into my stomach. This is unreal. My pulse pounds harder. I can't let him do this. "Sidney, her office door is locked. I can't take it back and I don't want to."

He's quiet for a moment and his hands release me. I can still feel his palm against my arm. I can't swallow. The moment passes slowly, as if time isn't real. Peter opens his mouth to say something. I do the same. Neither of us speaks. My skin is covered in chills that won't go away. I rub my hands over my arms, trying to chase the panicked feeling away, but it won't abate.

I'm scared out of my mind, and it's not the normal someone-is-hiding-under-the-bed scared, it's different. There are no hands strangling me, but I can't swallow. There is no tape over my mouth, but I can't breathe. There is no bullet in my heart, but I swear to God that it stops pounding. The weight of my gaze is pulled toward the ground. I can't lift my face. I can't look at him. Terror, fear, and joy all collide. I can't make my mouth form words. I'm twisting my hands so hard that they burn.

Peter's head hangs forward. Instead of giving his hands rope burn, his are shoved into his pockets. He inhales deeply, but his breaths are shaky. I wonder if he's as nervous as I am. This feels like one of those moments when everything matters. It's a crossroads where taking the wrong path will be devastating. I chose the wrong path once. It nearly destroyed me.

I glance back at the doors behind Peter. I can't let him do this. There's an ache that grows larger and larger in the center of my chest, as I think about what he's done and what it means. He gave up everything for me. My lips part and I'm about to speak, but he cuts me off.

His voice is so soft. "It's too late to take back your 'I love you.'" When he lifts his blue gaze, my hands start to shake. I hold them tighter, twisting them harder.

Looking straight into those haunted eyes, I say, "I'll never take that back. I love you. I love you so much."

"I love you, too. I'm sorry that I was so stupid. It took me way too long to do something."

I shake my head. "You shouldn't have."

Peter places his hands on my shoulders and steps toward me. Looking down into my face, pressing his forehead against mine, he says, "I had to. I couldn't lose you. Please tell me that I didn't lose you." Peter's eyes are lowered to my lips. He watches me for a second and I feel it.

This is the moment that matters. What I say now will change everything. He quit so he could be with me. He resigned. I feel so guilty and so glad. I'm an emotional train wreck. My engine is derailed and there's baggage everywhere—nightmares, worries, and regrets litter my mind. I've not felt like this about anyone. I never thought I'd have this chance. It was taken from me by someone I trusted. I wonder if I can really do it, if I can move on. I want to. I want to take the chance so badly I can feel it burning inside of me. Flames lick from my toes to my fingertips, urging me to move, to throw my arms around Peter and tell him how much he means to me.

But, I can't. I gasp and my gaze falls to his chest. There are so many reasons why. Each one clangs loudly inside my mind, vying for attention, promising nothing but pain. It's not that I don't want him, I do. It's that I know what this means, what that letter of resignation did. I could go back to his place right now. I could fall into his arms and let him love me until morning. I could show him how I feel about him. It's those thoughts that scare me. The door was opened. There's nothing holding us back, nothing keeping us apart. That makes it so much easier to see the obstacle blocking my path. I feel the scars burn, as if they might start bleeding. I'm not who I was. Pretending that I can be won't change things. I know now. I can't be with him, not that way. The thought terrifies me. Tears streak from the corners of my eyes. They sting and dampen my face. I open my mouth to say it, but Peter shakes his head. The look in his eyes rips me apart, but I have to say it. There's no future for us.

Peter steps back from me. "No. Don't say it. Sidney, give us a chance."

"I can't." My voice is barely a breath. "I can't be with you. I can't move on. And I can't take you down with me. I'm so sorry...So sorry." I grab my things and walk away with tears blurring my vision. Peter calls out, but he doesn't chase me down the steps. He watches me leave. He watches his biggest mistake walk away.

CHAPTER 23

I haven't said his name in years, not even inside my mind. It's like summoning him, and every bad thing that happened to me while I was with him, with Dean. I wipe the tears from my eyes with the back of my hands.

As I ran down the front steps, I felt Peter's eyes on me, but I didn't stop. I couldn't. I already ruined my life, I can't ruin his. By the time I get to the bottom of the massive staircase and turn back, Peter is gone. I never heard him leave, never heard the click of the doors. He left without a sound. It makes me want to cry more. My vision is blurry. I can't see a damn thing.

Yanking a tissue from my book bag, I fumble it and nearly drop everything on the ground. A few pens and Millie's pepper spray rolls out the side. I sweep them back in, not paying attention. I'm shaking. Every ounce of me wants to fall down on the grass and cry—cry because I'm too afraid to move forward, cry because I can't get over my past. I swallow hard and glance back up at the steps. Peter was willing to try.

But his pain is different, I think. *She didn't tie him to a seat and scratch his skin with his knife. She didn't press harder to see if he cried. She didn't use her strength to take what she wanted. She didn't do things like that. His pain is different. It has to be.*

I can't relive those nightmares. That's what being with Peter will do. I take a few breaths and steady myself. I drove over to this side of campus and need to get back to the dorm. I don't want glassy red eyes when I walk inside. Everyone will want to know what happened.

After wiping my face again, I start down the sidewalk. The sky is so dark that it's nearly black. There's no moon tonight. The few trees rustle in the breeze. There are some guys ahead, toward the opposite end of the street, next to the dorm. Most are moving toward the parking lot and getting into their cars. Some are in the field next to the building, playing football. A guy with no shirt on launches the ball. I watch it streak across the sky, and it isn't until my gaze follows the ball back down that I feel a prickling sensation on the back of my neck. I turn to see who's watching me, but there isn't anyone.

It seems as though I'm overly paranoid lately. I glance around, and my eyes go through the faces, most of which don't even realize I'm there. They're too far away, playing under the floodlights. I'm on the sidewalk in the shadows between lamp posts, two parking lots away from any of them.

Rubbing the hand over the back of my neck, I keep walking. My car is across the street. When I arrived, the main lot was full. I glance behind me one more time. I wonder where Peter went. Regret washes over me. I didn't want to hurt him. God, the look on his face when I said 'no' was too much. I reach into my bag, feeling around for my keys, as I cross the street. When I'm out of the crosswalk, I hop onto the sidewalk and head into the parking lot. I'm several rows back, but it's fairly empty tonight. Where are my keys? I pull my bag in front of me and shift things around, trying to find them. Everything is out of place from dropping the bag.

"You look as beautiful now as you did the day you ran away."

That voice. My spine straightens. Every little hair on my neck stands on end. I nearly drop my bag as I look around for him. My fight or flight kicks in and my feet want to run, but fear holds me in place. It can't be Dean. Why would he be here? But it is him. It's the same voice from my nightmares. It's a voice that I'll never forget.

I don't find my keys. I'm suddenly aware of how much air I'm breathing, and the way my skin is prickling. Little bumps form on my arms when I see Dean standing against the side of the building. My chest constricts. I have no words. I want to run, but for some reason I don't move.

He pushes off the wall and walks toward me. "Damn fine way to say hello. Hello, Sidney," he says stopping in front of me. "Then, you say 'hello, Dean.'"

I manage to find my voice. "What are you doing here?" It's Texas. I'm thousands of miles from home, hidden in a little town in a vast state.

Dean gives me a smile that makes my blood run cold. It's the same look he had in his eye before he—

I push away the memories, but they won't be tamed. I'm suddenly there again. It's four years ago. Dean has a knife on my thigh. I can't make a sound or he'll cut me. I lay perfectly still, letting him use me however he wants. Another memory flies forward, from when the tiniest whimper left my lips. I feel the pain sear my neck like he just did it. There were too many times. I shiver and try to force them back, but I can't, not with Dean standing there.

"Nice way to say hello. You were always a bit of bitch, weren't you?" His eyes drop to my breasts as he speaks. They linger there too long before returning to my face. "Just the way I like it." He steps toward me. He touches my forearm, runs his finger along my skin. I choke, but it's silent. I make no sound because that's what he conditioned me to do.

We're standing a few spaces away from my car. My book bag is hanging off my shoulder. No one is nearby. *I can't. I can't. I can't*, is replaying over and over again in my mind, but I say nothing. I'm frozen.

Dean's hands touch my skin lightly, trailing a sickening path up to my neck. He pushes my chin to the side and lifts the chain around my neck. He grins. "It scarred." He looks into my eyes and grins. "Fun times, huh, Colleli?" He drops the chain and steps back.

Dean strokes his chin and shakes his head. "Damn shame we don't have time right now. I'd love to fuck the way we used to, but I promised your brother that we'd meet up with him as soon as I found you." Dean grins at me. His eyes sweep over my body and it feels as if I've been raped all over again. He pulls a phone from his pocket and texts someone.

I find my brain and what little sense of self-preservation I have left. "My brother's here?"

Dean nods. "Yeah. Some family shit is going on. We're here to take you home."

My mouth opens and I'm shaking my head. Why is that worse than seeing Dean? Having Dean and Sam drag me home is unthinkable. "No, you're not. I live here, asshole. I'm not going anywhere with you." I push past him, trying to get to my car.

Dean's hand shoots out. He grips my arm hard and jerks me back. I'm standing right in front of him. "I'm afraid that you don't have a say in the matter, but I like the spine you grew while you've been down here." He yanks me, turning me around so my back is to him. "It looks great with that tight little ass."

I kick at him, and try to pull my arm back. "Let go of me! I'm not going with you."

Dean laughs. His grip on my arm tightens. "How sweet. You think you get a say in this. Well, you don't. Get in the fucking truck." I nearly fall over when I look up and see where he's leading me. It's the Explorer he used to drive, the same one where he did all those things to me. My knees go weak. I fall. My bag hits the ground next to me and the contents spill out. Pens, pencils, and papers go everywhere. The wind takes the pages and blows them down the street like they're snowflakes.

My eyes are too wide. My lips are parted. The voice in my head keeps telling me to scream, but I can't. I have no air. It's as if someone hit me in the back with a board.

"Get up and get into the goddamn truck before I throw you in." Dean pulls at me, but I'm dead weight slumped on the ground in a heap. He pulls harder, twisting my arm. I yelp and look up at him. "I'll break it. I swear to God. Get up and get in the truck."

I don't move.

Dean twists my arm behind my back, hard. A scream rips from my throat. The pain that is shooting through me and into my shoulder is blinding. My gaze falls to the ground. Dean is talking, saying things that I can't hear. He releases me, but the fire inside my bones doesn't stop burning.

Dean pushes me with his shoe, yells at me. "Shut the fuck up. People are going to get the wrong idea." Dean pulls me up by my other arm and drags me. When he's nearly there, he lifts me onto his shoulder like I'm a child. He's going to throw me inside.

I freak out. My brain snaps and goes Cujo on his ass. My teeth sink into his shoulder and I bite down. His shirt tastes of blood and I bite down harder. Dean screams, cursing, and throws me. My back hits the ground first. White spots form around the edges of my vision, making it hard to see. Unbelievable pain shoots up my arm and into my shoulder. It's a million times worse than before.

I'm screaming. I don't even know what I'm saying, but I start repeating, "Leave me alone!" over and over again. When Dean tries to pick me up, I kick at him. My foot connects with his face.

"You fucking whore!" Dean is holding his cheek, growling at me. "I'm going to make you pay for that." He's coming at me again. I stay down and kick at him. Dean dodges my feet and manages to grab my ankle. He drags me toward his truck. I twist around and try to crawl away. The asphalt shreds my palms to bits.

"Stop! Let me go!" I'm screaming. I'm trying to fight back. I am not getting in that truck. I manage to twist my hips quickly and roll onto my back again. I kick hard and my heel jabs him in the balls.

As soon as Dean's hand is off my ankle, I roll over and crawl back to my bag. I find my keys, but before I can get up and run to my car, he hits me. Dean's hand strikes the side of my face. The keys go flying. I'm sobbing and screaming. Snot and blood are mixing together. Dean is holding my face so hard that I can't pull away. My teeth are biting into my cheek drawing blood. I taste it inside my mouth.

Dean's brow is covered in sweat. He hisses in my face, "Get into the truck and I'll make this easy on you. Keep fighting back and your ride home will be much less enjoyable. Do you understand what I'm telling you?" One hand is on my face, holding me tight. The other slips between my legs, over my jeans, and he grabs me.

Instinct takes over. I'm not the same girl I was four years ago. I'd rather die than let him touch me again. I slam my head into his nose and hear it crack. Blood gushes everywhere. Dean growls so deeply that he sounds more animal than human.

I'm running. I have no idea what I'm going to do, but I run back toward the English building. Halfway down the sidewalk I run straight into Peter. My body slams into his. He steadies me, holding my shoulders and I cry out.

Peter's eyes narrow and a look of fury spreads across his face when he notices the blood. It's everywhere. "What happened?"

"He's here. Behind me in the parking lot." I can barely breathe.

Peter drops his things and pulls out his cell, punches in a number, but the call doesn't connect fast enough. He's looking around. He doesn't see them, but I do. I stiffen in Peter's arms. Sam and Dean are walking towards us. Peter is dressed in his suit pants and white button down shirt. His jacket is draped over his bag. He doesn't look threatening.

Sam and Dean grin at each other when they see me with him. Peter steps in front of me. "What's going on? Which one of you did this to her?"

Sam throws my bag at my feet. "Cut it out, Sidney. It's time to go. Pick up your shit and get in the truck."

"I'm not going with you." I wipe my face with the back of my hand.

"It's not an option," Sam says, his eyes flashing a warning at me.

"She isn't going with you," Peter repeats.

Sam steps toward Peter. "I'm her brother. I drove down here to get her and bring her home. Our mom needs her. I guess she didn't recognize Dean." He looks over at his friend and laughs. "She must have thought you were a mugger or something. She beat the shit out of you, man. Sid didn't even recognize her old boyfriend." He turns back to Peter and acts like what just occurred is normal and could have happened to anyone. Sam holds out his hand, gesturing for me to come. "Let's get going. It's a long drive back."

"You're her brother?" Peter asks. Sam looks at me and then nods. "And you're her ex?" Dean is holding his shirt to his nose, trying to stop the bleeding.

"Yeah, that's what he said, shithead." Dean says it to Peter, but he's staring at me like he intends to rip me apart once we're alone.

Peter's voice is so deep that it rumbles. His shoulders tense. He only says two words. "Leave. Now."

Dean laughs and looks at Sam, and then back at Peter. "Or what?" Dean steps in front of Sam and keeps talking. He's so close to Peter. "You'll write me up? Any chance you have a little crush on my girl? Because she is my girl, Sidney will always be mine." He grins at me and my insides go cold. "Did she tell you that we used to be an item? Did she tell you that she likes some messed up shit?"

Peter doesn't respond. His hands are at his sides. The only reason that I can tell that he's upset is the way his fingers twitch every few seconds, as if he's.

Dean gazes past Peter, and gives me a look that makes me sick inside. "Or did you already do her?"

Peter doesn't answer.

Sam is annoyed, "Cut it out, Dean. I don't want to hear what shit my sister does in bed." He snaps his fingers at me like I'm a dog. "Come. Now."

"Aren't you going to answer me?" Dean smirks and presses his finger tips to Peter's chest. "Or are you just pissed because she won't sleep with you." He pushes Peter again. Harder this time.

Peter moves. In two steps he's behind Dean with his arm around his throat. Peter's hissing in Dean's ear, saying things too low for me to hear. Dean claws at his throat. He swings his elbow back, but doesn't do it hard enough to make Peter let go.

"What the fuck?" Sam yells. He gives me a look that I recognize all too well—*this is your fault.* Sam throws a punch and hits Peter in the side. Peter lets go of Dean. Sam and Dean go at him.

I scream, bellowing like a banshee. I can't stop. The players down field stop and look toward us.

The three guys are fighting, but it seems as though Peter is getting overpowered. I don't know what to do. There are a few guys from the field hurrying towards us. Peter lands a hit on Sam's face. Something cracks. Sam drops back, yelling. Dean doesn't stop. His knife, that fucking knife, is in his hand. Peter's eyes lock on the knife and he backs away. Sam moves and is telling Dean to put it away, but Dean doesn't. He jabs it forward, narrowly missing Peter.

No, no, no. My bag is on the sidewalk. I see it, that silver pen, the one Millie gave me this morning. I race toward it and pick it up. I'm so nervous that I can barely line up the cap with the mark on the side. It isn't a pen. It's her pepper spray. I shake the thing as I rush back toward Dean and Peter.

Peter sees me coming. I spray my brother. He screams and rubs his eyes, cursing at me. When Dean turns to see what's happened, the stream of liquid hits him in the face. Dean yells, clawing at his face and doubles over, dropping the knife. I kick it into the drainage ditch and tug at Peter.

"Take me home. Now." I grab my bag, Peter grabs his, and we're running toward his car. The field full of guys sees us run past. They don't say anything. I recognize Mark. He sees my face, the blood. His eyes widen before they narrow. He pulls out his phone. I see him talking as we pull away.

CHAPTER 24

Peter is breathing hard, his hand clutching the wheel. We're driving away from the college. "Are you hurt?"

My head is against the seat. My eyes are pinched shut. I nod. "My shoulder. I think it's not in the socket."

"Hold on a few minutes more, okay? I can fix that. I'll get you some pain medicine and you can call the cops from my place." He pulls into the parking lot and he helps me up the stairs. Peter has a cut on his cheek, but he looks pretty good. Me on the other hand, I look like hell.

When he sees me in the light, Peter nearly has a coronary. "You're bleeding."

"Most of it is his, not mine. I think I broke his nose with my face." I rub my forehead. "My head hurts. It feels like my brain is in a vice." We're in his apartment. I'm standing in his living room with panic dripping through me. The feelings are still raging through me even though I'm safe.

Peter hands me Advil. I take them and swallow the pills down. Peter explains what he's going to do to my shoulder because that does seem to be the problem. I tell him to do it. I cry out when it pops back in. "That hurt just as much as pulling it out." I rub my arm. There are tears in my eyes.

"What happened?" Peter's hands are on me, gently sliding down my face, my arms. He's so careful. "What did he do to you? Did he—"

"No," I breathe. My pulse is finally slowing down. "He said stuff and grabbed me. He didn't do anything else, besides try and shove me in his truck. All this happened because I wouldn't just go with him."

Peter's fingers touch the ends of my hair. "You fought back. Good girl." He takes a deep breath and reaches for the phone. "I'll call it in."

I take his hands and stop him. "No, don't."

Peter looks up at me. "Sidney, you need to report this."

"Sam didn't do anything. It was Dean."

"Sam chose to help the wrong person. You don't owe him anything."

"He's my brother. Peter, please. Let me think about it. I can't decide right now. Please don't, not right now."

He watches me for a moment and nods. "Let me look you over." He takes my hands and looks at my nails. A few of them are ripped all the way into the nail bed. Peter turns my hands over and looks at my scraped palms. When he looks back up at me, his eyes are filled with remorse. "I shouldn't have left you alone."

"You didn't know."

"I could have…" his voice drifts off. Peter shakes his head and turns away. I sit down on the couch. Exhaustion is creeping up on me. Peter goes to the bathroom and comes back with the first aid kit and towels. He's breathing too hard. Peter doesn't look at my face. He takes my hands and turns them so the palms are up. His touch makes me feel so much better.

My vision is blurry, but I finally look at his face. The cut on his cheek is deep. It looks like a piece of metal tore the skin away. I look down. Peter's hands are roughed up, too. There are too many things to say. I want to explain why I said no before. Even if I never saw Dean again, I'd be dealing with this for the rest of my life. "Peter, about earlier…"

"There's nothing to say. I understand. It's fine." He pours peroxide over my cuts and I flinch. His voice is cold, like he doesn't want to talk about it, so I don't. I nod. I'm a coward. After a moment, he asks, "Why did they want to take you home?"

"I don't know. They didn't say anything except that Mom sent them."

He nods slowly, tending to my other hand. "Do you want to go home?"

I look down at him as if that was the stupidest thing he could have asked. "No, I don't."

"Even if it was just your brother?"

I stiffen. "My brother thinks I like rough sex and that I was asking for it. He doesn't think that Dean hurt me. He doesn't believe that his friend used me." My jaw locks. I'm defensive and I don't know why. I feel like Peter is saying what Dean said. I can't handle it. "Is that what you think? You think that I liked it, that I wanted it?" My arms are so tense that they jerk out of Peter's grip. I stand up and walk down the hall, not knowing where I'm going. I want to scream.

Peter's behind me. His voice is soft, soothing "I know that isn't true, Sidney. I know. I wish I could change it. I wish I could take away some of your pain. Sometimes, family helps, that's all. I wanted to make sure you weren't throwing away your hand to spite your arm."

I glare at him. "Fuck you." My entire body is shaking with rage. "You think I don't know how I feel about this? You think that I haven't laid there every night since it happened wondering if I did this to myself? If all that shit he said was true? I thought it was. For a long time, I thought I did it, that I led him on. That's why it kept happening and every time was worse than the last. I let him rape, cut, and burn me. I let him do it over and over again. My parents loved him. They didn't defend me. My brother didn't even believe me, so don't pretend that you know a damn thing about it because you don't. You have no fucking clue!"

I'm screaming. My hands are clenching into balls at my sides and I can't stop. I want to stop. I don't want things to be like this, but my mouth keeps going. Peter's eyes fall to the floor. He can't even look at me. I try so hard to stop shaking. My muscles are so tense, so tight. I have to control this. I have to hold myself together, but I can't. I feel the patches unraveling. I feel the weight of my pain tearing me apart. My bottom lip quivers. I bite it, but it doesn't stop. A sob bubbles up my throat. I turn away from Peter. I can't stand this. I can't stand that he sees this version of me. That's why I said no. That's why I turned him away. No matter what I do, this part of me will always be there. I bury my face in my hands and push the tears away.

Peter walks up behind me. His hand touches my shoulder gently. He turns me toward him as he speaks. "I don't know what you've been through. I don't have a clue. I don't understand. I can't even pretend to…"

I stare at his chest, at his bloody shirt. My hand reaches for him before I realize what I'm doing. It laces around his waist and I lean into his chest. Peter's arms fold around me. He holds me and lets me cry. He lets me mourn everything I've lost without making offers to fix something that he can't. Peter lets me weep a river of tears and holds me close.

Eventually, I notice his heartbeat. I listen to it thumping in his chest. It stills me, steadies me. I press my lips together too many times before asking, "Can I stay here tonight?" I'm afraid he'll say no. I'm afraid I've ruined everything and that he doesn't want me here anymore.

When he speaks, his voice is soft. "Of course." His hand strokes the back of my head. Peter holds me until I let go. Then, he gives me towels and turns on the shower. He lays an oversized tee shirt on the bathroom counter. "I don't really have any women's clothes, but that should be good enough for tonight."

I nod and he leaves me alone.

CHAPTER 25

The scent of Peter fills my head as I lay in his bed. The room is warm and quiet. Peter's arms are around me and he's asleep. His gentle, slow, breathing makes me feel safe. It keeps away the horrors that happened tonight. They're fighting for me to replay the memories over and over again, which is why I don't sleep. I don't want to close my eyes. I don't want to remember.

I'm on my back. Peter's arm is draped across my stomach. I'm so tired. I watch him breathe, watch his chest rise and fall. Peter came to bed with a pair of pajama pants and no shirt. My eyes trace his muscles lazily. I wonder what it must be like for him, to be down here alone, and then run into a train wreck like me.

He's too good to me, too kind. Peter gave me his love and I threw it back in his face. He stirs and turns on his side. His hand drops to the bed between us. It makes his hips turn toward me. My eyes travel over his body, and rest on a jagged white scar at his waist. It's nearly on his back, but not quite. Seeing it makes my stomach sink. Something happened to him. It's not a surgical scar. It can't be. The line looks more like a Jack-O-Lantern's smile than anything else.

As I'm staring, Peter's eyes open. His tired gaze meets mine. Peter blinks slowly. "Are you still up?"

"Yeah." Now that he's awake, I'm nervous. My life is such a mess that I feel as though there isn't any room for him in it. But...

Peter holds open his arms and says, "Come here." I do as he says. I scoot over to him and lay on his chest. Peter holds onto me. His body is so warm, so strong. I close my eyes and he strokes the back of my head. I moan without meaning too. He smiles. "You like that?"

"Mmmm," I manage to reply. My mind tries to drift. Peter's scent fills my head. My heart knows it's where it needs to be, but my mind is at war with itself. It has a million reasons why we shouldn't be together, a million more about how much I'll hurt him. I mean, I'm lying with the man in his bed and have no desire to have sex. There's nothing. No tingles, no anything.

"Stop thinking. Go to sleep."

"What makes you think I'm—"

"Your only comment should be Mmmmm." He rubs my head harder and I moan again. I giggle just a little. It sounds foreign to me, but not unwelcome. "That was cute. You can do that too."

I mutter something, not thinking, and curl into him. Peter rubs my head until I drift off.

———

When I open my eyes, I have no idea where I am. I dart upright, taking the sheet with me. Peter is next to me. He blinks himself awake. I turn and look at him. I woke him up. Again. What time is it? I glance around for a clock. "It's after nine!" I've missed my morning class. I go to throw my legs over the side of the bed and get up, but Peter takes my hand.

"Stay with me."

Nerves lace up my neck and choke me. It's the same thing I asked him last night. I think about it, but my mind is screaming to run. I'll ruin everything. It's not fair, though. And last night meant so much to me. He took care of me, he protected me. If Peter hadn't shown up, I'd be in Tennessee by now.

I smile at him. Peter smiles back.

"Okay." I lay back down, but I feel nervous. I'm more aware of everything today, of his bed, of his cologne, of him. I try not to think about it. I try to stop the jitters that are working their way up my arms. I pull up the sheet, covering myself. "So, what do you want to do?"

Peter lifts a brow. "First, I want to tell you that I'm glad you aren't hurt and that I think you should call the cops. But since I know you don't want to, I think we should have some coffee."

My face pales. Is he joking? I manage to choke out, "What?"

Peter looks at me funny, and then laughs. "No! Not like that. I mean real coffee, in real cups, and everything." He's still smiling. Reaching for me, Peter tucks a curl behind my ear. "What do you think?"

"It sounds good, as long as we're being literal." I smile, feeling shy. When I glance up at him my eyes fall on the scar by his waist.

Peter's smile vanishes. "I forgot about that." He rolls onto his back and covers his face with his hands and rubs. "You want to know what happened, right?"

"A little bit…"

He pushes onto his side and pulls up the sheet so I can't see the marred skin. "I want to know some things about you."

The way he says it makes me worried. But I want him to say whatever he's thinking. "Go ahead and ask."

"Last night you said something—that your ex cut you. I didn't realize that." Peter looks into my eyes. His fingers trail along my cheek as he speaks. "If you don't want to talk about it—"

"There's not much to say. He was twisted. He'd tie me up and tell me not to yell. That was the first time. It gave him a rush, I guess. I kind of thought it was fun at first. I didn't know what he was going to do and it made my heart race faster. He used to kiss me, after he tied my hands, but then one day he didn't. He changed things. He slid his knife down my hip and said that he'd cut me if I screamed." My eyes dart to the side. I can't look at Peter while I say it. "He took things further one day. His hand went down my pants while he hand the knife to my neck. It scared me. I made a sound and he…" I take a breath.

"You don't have to tell me."

"I haven't told anyone, not really. My parents didn't hear all of it." I shrug. Nerves are swimming in my stomach. "Maybe telling someone will help me get over it." Peter smiles at me, but it's sad, like he knows what I mean. I finish the story. "He nicked me, here." I point to my neck. There's a scar that sits at the base of my throat, right by my collar bone.

I take a deep breath and ask, "Where'd the scar on your side come from?"

"A knife. It came from a knife." Peter's quiet for a moment. Then he starts telling me. "It's from the night I proposed. I was down on one knee. Gina had her hands to her mouth, surprised, and smiling so big. She was looking at me, at the ring I held out. We were talking, saying things. She didn't get to answer me…" His eyes glaze over while he speaks. I can almost see the memory in his eyes. "I felt a sharp pain in my side as the ring was grabbed out of my hand. Some guys had been watching us. They did it. The guy that stabbed me twisted the knife. That's why it looks like that."

I can't breathe. There are tears in my eyes. "Oh, my God. Peter…"

We're both quiet for a moment. Then Peter asks, "Want to keep going?" I don't know why, but I nod. His eyes flick up to mine. "Are you afraid to have sex after everything that happened?"

My face flames red. My mouth opens and snaps shut again. "I want to say no. I want to say something, anything, else, but I can't." I look at him, wondering what I should say, if I should tell him how messed up I am. Dean broke me. I can't imagine being normal anymore. Even when I was sitting with Peter the first day I met him, it wasn't the way it's supposed to be.

I smile, but my lips won't hold it. They twitch instead. "I'm not afraid to have sex. It's not the action, well, not totally. I'm afraid that I won't like it. I'm afraid my mind will be stuck in the past somewhere and not here with you.

"As it is, I don't feel like it, not really. I laid here next to you all night, and I don't know if you know this or not, but you're kind of hot." He smiles. His eyes lock with mine and hold my gaze. I want to tell him everything. "I didn't feel like it. I never seem to want more than kisses or your hands on my face. When I think about other things," I shiver and shake my head. I press my lips together nervously and look up at him. "I can't image feeling that way again. And last time was such a horrible mistake, how will I know? What if I make the same mistake again? What if…what if you hurt me?"

Peter takes my hand and pulls it to his lips. He kisses the center of my palm and looks into my eyes. "I will never, ever, hurt you like that."

"How can I know that for sure? Dean didn't start out that way, I mean—"

He holds my hand between his and looks me in the eye. "I *am* sure. I'm not like that. Most guys aren't like that. That isn't love, Sidney. He was using you."

I can't swallow. I nod a little too frantically. "Can you prove that you aren't?"

He shakes his head. "I don't think so, other than showing you how I feel about you. I love you. If you wanted to be with me, I'd wait for you. We don't have to have sex, not right away, and not until you're ready."

I feel sick inside. I can't look at him. My voice is weak, "I'll never be ready."

"Then, I'll always be waiting." He smiles at me and leans forward and kisses my nose. It makes me look up at him. My eyelashes flutter too much and I smile. "I'll do anything for you, be anything you need. I just don't want to let you go."

CHAPTER 26

I must have dozed off because I wake up again a few hours later. Peter is talking on the other side of the bedroom door. It's cracked, letting a little bit of light from the hallway spill inside. I stretch and push back the covers. My hands hurt. I forgot they were torn up. Stretching reminds me that my body will not be my friend today. I ache all over.

Rubbing my eyes, I pad across the room to the door. I watch Peter for a second. He has the phone to his ear and he's talking softly.

"I know what it means." He pauses and pushes his hair back, away from his eyes. His brow is pinched. "There's more to it than that. Have you ever found someone that sees right through you? When she looks at me... It's like we were thrown together, like my life didn't turn into a pile of shit for no reason. I can't leave her. I don't expect you to understand. I just wanted you to know that it wasn't a whim." Peter shakes his head as if he can't handle what the other person is saying. "I won't be coming back, but thank you all the same. I'll come by later and empty out my office." He takes the phone from his ear and presses a button, then tosses it on the table.

I feel bad for watching him. Peter senses me. He turns and sees me standing in the doorway. "Hey. Feel any better?"

I give a weak smile and walk toward him. "A little bit. Thanks for letting me sleep." I look at him, wondering who he was talking to. Peter seems rattled. "Are you all right?"

His eyes meet mine. He doesn't say anything for a moment. Then he takes a slow breath and says, "They want me to come back."

"Who?" I look up at him. I already know who, but I want to make sure.

"The University. That was Strictland. She said that she didn't file my resignation, that I'm making a mistake." Peter runs his hands through his hair and then down his neck. He sighs and looks straight at me.

I feel guilty. My stomach twists. I didn't want this. I'm messing up his life. "You guys sound close." I wonder about that.

He nods. "We were at the same university when I did my undergrad. Before she relocated here, Strictland oversaw my internships and wrote my recommendations for grad school. I was her TA, too. I got to know her since I was around her every day. That's how I got the job here. She shoulder tapped me for another position. When Tadwick passed away, she moved me into his classroom." He folds his arms over his chest. When he looks at me again, he adds, "I was kind of close to Strictland back then. She knew me before everything happened."

My eyes dart to his side, to that scar, but it's covered by a white tee shirt. When my gaze flicks back to his face, I nod. "You should go back." He laughs, like he thinks I'm kidding. "I'm serious, Peter. I can't do this to you. I—"

"You didn't. Some asshole in New York did this to me. Someone they didn't even find stole my life from me. It wasn't you. If anything, you gave me a second chance." He sighs and steps toward me. Peter takes my hand and pulls me to the couch. I follow, feeling a little more than exposed in my tee shirt. We sit down. He turns toward me. "I need to know what you want to do about last night."

I bristle. "I'm not calling the police."

He shakes his head and takes my hand. He pulls it into his lap. "That's not what I mean. Do you want to—?"

Before he can finish, there's a loud thud as someone pounds on the door. I know who it is before he speaks. "Open the goddamn door! I know she's in there." Sam' voice fills the room.

Peter looks at me and then back at the door. The pounding stops. Silence follows. The door is a few feet away. Peter gets up and looks out the peep hole, then comes back to me.

"It's your brother. Do you want me to let him in?" Peter's voice is tight. His fingers flex into fists and reopen.

"Dean's not there?" Peter shakes his head. I don't know what to do. I don't want to talk to Sam, but I have to get him to leave me alone. "Wait a second." I get up and find my jeans. I pull them on under Peter's shirt and smooth my hair a little bit. This is going to look wrong, but I realize that I don't care what he thinks. Sam pounds on the door again. I nod at Peter and he opens it. Sam's hand flies through the air when the door is suddenly yanked open.

Peter glares at him. "If you try to take her again, I will kick your ass."

Sam smirks. "Like last night? If I recall correctly, my sister saved your ass."

Peter is through being nice. I can see something snap inside of him. Instead of answering, Peter grabs Sam by the throat and pushes him into the wall hard. He hisses something in his ear that I can't hear. Sam's eyes widen. His face is turning red.

He can't breathe. Peter drops my brother, then slams the front door shut.

Peter folds his chiseled arms over his chest and says, "You have two minutes. Talk."

Sam is leery of Peter. I can tell that he doesn't like this, that he doesn't want to talk in front of Peter, but he does anyway. "Sorry about Dean."

"Don't apologize. I don't want to hear it. What do you want?" I snap. We're both standing, staring at each other. He's my twin. We were so close once. He knew what I thought and how I felt, but I don't know him anymore. He chose his jackass friend over me. I fold my arms over my chest and stare at him. Sam's eyes cut to the side. He glances at Peter. "Just say it."

Sam looks at my shoes. He's silent.

The little muscles on the side of Peter's jaw are twitching. He says, "One minute."

Sam scowls at Peter. "It hasn't been a minute! What the fuck, man?"

"I don't care and you're wasting your time." Peter glares at him.

Sam finally says something, and gives me an indication as to why he's here.

"Mom's sick, like really sick. She's been asking for you. I told her that I'd find you and bring you home. You can't send me back without you. Please, sis. She's dying."

I don't want this news to affect me, but it does. My arms drop to my sides. "When? How long has this been going on?"

He tilts his head to the side. It's his *are you a moron* face. "I sent you letters. It got a lot worse a few months ago. I found you last Christmas. I knew something wasn't right, but I didn't want to make Mom worse. When she started asking for you, I started writing you, asking you to come home. Way to blow me off."

I watch him. There are too many emotions boiling beneath the surface. "I didn't open the letters."

"Why the fuck not?"

I glare at him. "You seriously want me to answer that? You're dead to me, all of you. I don't want anything to do with any of you. And why the hell are you still hanging out with Dean? Look what he did to me last night! Look!" I hold up my hands so he can see my palms. They're covered in scabs. "This is nothing compared to what he used to do. How could you bring him here?"

"You're still on that?"

"Holy fuck," Peter turns and yells in Sam's face. "Are you that stupid? Look at your sister and tell me that she liked getting her skin ripped off last night. Say it, asshole." Peter pushes Sam's shoulders, but Sam doesn't push back. Whatever Peter said to him before still has Sam spooked.

Sam's eyes flick to mine. "Just come home." He turns and leaves without another word. Peter shuts the door behind him. When Peter turns to look at me, I feel like I'm falling apart. I don't understand how or why I even care. I have no more tears. I reach behind me, and fall down onto the couch nauseated.

"Why? Why did he have to come here and tell me that? I can't go. I can't face them. Not after everything that happened." I'm taking to myself, saying a million reasons why I can't do it.

After a few moments, I feel Peter sit down next to me. I'm staring straight ahead, seeing nothing. I don't know what to do, and I don't know why. "There's only one question here, Sidney. Will you regret not saying good-bye to your mom?"

"I don't know. I can't face them. I can't manage them and Dean, and…"

"I'll go with you." I glance up at him, surprised. "You don't think I'd send you alone? Not with those two?"

"What'd you say to him?"

Peter grins wickedly, and shakes his head. "Not telling. That's my little secret. I was holding back last night. I didn't want to hurt either of them. I didn't want to cause you more pain or make you feel more conflicted about me than you already do. I warned Sam that I won't hold back again. No one will hurt you, not while I'm around." His eyes are so blue.

"I don't want this life. I want a refund." I grip my face in my hands. I don't know what to do. Part of me wants to go. My mom has never said she needed me before. If she really said that, I should go, but I don't know if Sam is lying.

Peter wraps his arms around me and pulls me to his chest. "I don't want a refund." His words shock me. Peter's been through hell and back. I sit up and look at him.

"You'd do it over again?"

He nods. "In a heartbeat."

"Why?" My mouth drops open into a little O. I can't stand my life. I'd trade it in a second. I feel like a piece of tissue paper that's been torn and glued back together too many times. There's no tissue left. All the color is gone. I'm a mass of scars and glue. The pieces of me that remain are battered and broken.

I watch Peter's face. I don't understand how he can say that he'd knowingly sign up for this.

He smiles at me and touches my cheek. "I wouldn't give any of it up. I know who I am. I know what matters to me. Those things shaped me, they changed me. I wouldn't do it differently. I wouldn't give it up." He leans in close to me, his lips right by mine. He whispers to me, "And, I'd do it exactly the same way again if I was given another chance, because in the end, it led me to you."

Peter's courage gives me strength. I didn't know I felt this way. I didn't think that I could take my life back, not after having it violently ripped away.

I know what I need to do. Running away didn't work. My past found me. It will always find me. I'll never be free, not unless I face the pain I tried to leave behind.

I have to go home and face my past.

DAMAGED #2

Coming Soon!

To ensure you don't miss DAMAGED #2, text **AWESOMEBOOKS** to **22828** and you will get an email reminder on release day.

MORE ROMANCE BOOKS BY
H.M. WARD

THE ARRANGEMENT

SCANDALOUS

SCANDALOUS 2

SECRETS

THE SECRET LIFE OF TRYSTAN
SCOTT

And more.

To see a full book list, please visit:

www.SexyAwesomeBooks.com/books.htm

**CAN'T WAIT FOR H.M WARD'S
NEXT STEAMY BOOK?**

Let her know by leaving stars and
telling her what you liked about
DAMAGED in a review!

Made in the USA
Lexington, KY
01 December 2014